THE DEMON KISS

RITE WORLD: BLACKTHORN HUNTERS
ACADEMY BOOK 1

JULIANA HAYGERT

COPYRIGHT

AUTHOR'S NOTE

I hope you enjoy reading *The Demon Kiss*!

Don't forget to sign up for my Newsletter to find out about new releases, cover reveals, giveaways, and more!

If you want to see exclusive teasers, help me decide on covers, read excerpts, talk about books, etc, join my reader group on Facebook: Juliana's Club!

RITE WORLD

Welcome to the RITE WORLD!

Free Novella:
The Vampire Hunt

Rite World:
The Vampire Heir (Book 1)
The Witch Queen (Book 2)
The Immortal Vow (Book 3)
The Warlock Lord (Book 4)
The Wolf Consort (Book 5)
The Crystal Rose (Book 6)
The Wolf Forsaken (Book 7)
The Fae Bound (Book 8)
The Blood Pact (Book 9)

Rite World: Blackthorn Hunters Academy
The Demons Kiss (Book 1)

The Hunter Secret (Book 2)
The Soul Bond (Book 3)
The Shadow Trials (Book 4)
The Immortal Vow (Book 5)

And more to come!

THE VAMPIRE HUNT

I have an exclusive novella set in the Rite World that is just for my newsletter subscribers!

Click here to sign-up and receive your book!

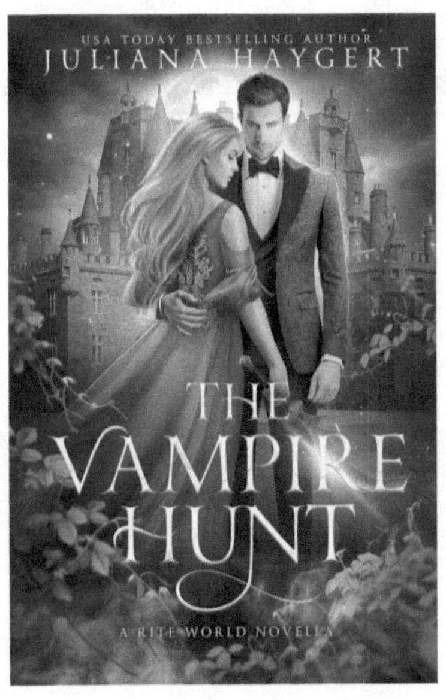

THE VAMPIRE HUNT
A Rite World Novella

Norah is a demon hunter, one of the best graduated from the Blackthorn Hunters Academy. When she's sent to investigate a case concerning demons in a small town, she runs into a very arrogant vampire. Her first instinct is to kill him, after all, he's a supernatural and demon hunters are taught to end all evil.

Cain is a vampire prince. Because of his status, he's in charge of making sure humans don't find out about his kind. During a routine investigation, he bumps into a very sexy demon hunter and he wonders what she's doing on his way.

However, the case grows much bigger for Norah and Cain to handle alone. To find the truth and win this battle, the vampire and the demon hunter will have to hunt together—without killing each other.

How well could this end?

MAP

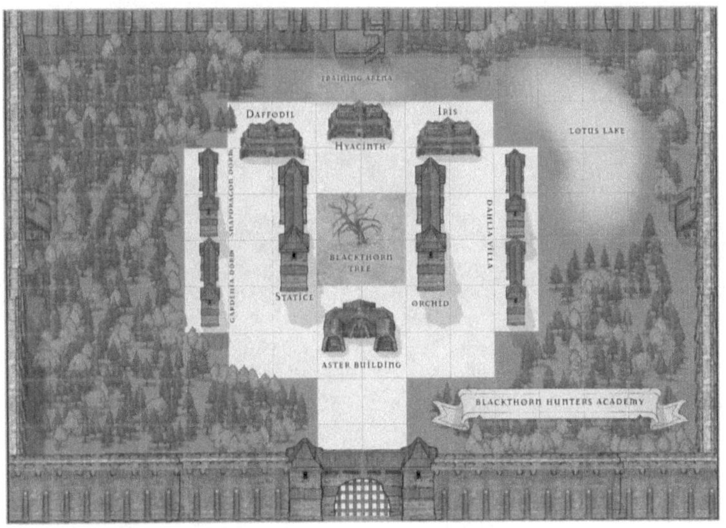

Map of Blackthorn Hunters Academy

Click here to view the map in a separate browser.

1

ERIN

THE RIDE TO THE HAUNTED HOUSE WAS QUIET.

Well, on my part. Mike drove his fancy Mercedes, with Karla in the passenger seat, and Noah and Alisha in the back with me. In the twenty minutes it took to drive from Spring Hill to the base of the mountain, they didn't stop talking about their college plans, all the parties they would go to, all the fun they would have, and all the studying they would avoid.

I kept my eyes trained on the darkening sky, across the Colorado mountains, wondering what the hell I was doing. Seriously, what had gotten into me? It wasn't like me to do something crazy like this.

But now that I was here, I couldn't chicken out. I would go through with this ridiculous game, get my money, and go home fifteen hundred dollars richer.

When Mike turned onto a dirt-packed road, I knew we were close. I fished my phone from the pocket of my blouse and texted my aunt.

Me: *I'll be late tonight.*

A moment later, my phone vibrated.

Aunt Paula: *Why? Is everything okay?*

Of course, she would think something was wrong. I had no friends and never did anything other than staying home and checking on her at work. I had never stayed out late, except for when I was craving ice cream from the food truck that sometimes stayed open past midnight near the main square during the summer.

Me: *Yeah. Everything is fine. See you later.*

Aunt Paula: *Later.*

I was sure that, by now, my aunt had come up with fifteen ridiculous scenarios, trying to figure out why I was suddenly out. Like the hidden college applications in my bedroom, she would kill me if she found out where I was going and with whom.

When I was little, I had a phase when I couldn't sleep at night. I thought there was a monster living in my closet. My aunt had been adamant that such things didn't exist. When I watched horror movies and became afraid, she would yell at me, saying it was all make believe.

Ghosts and any kinds of supernaturals didn't exist, she always said.

It took me a while, but I became convinced she was right by the time I was a teenager.

As for the group I was currently with, my aunt didn't like them much. She had had some heated arguments with Karla's mother and with Noah's older brother. She always complained the rich people of Spring Hill didn't know how to spend their money and wasted it on useless stuff. She thought they were vain, selfish, and arrogant.

I thought so too.

A moment later, Mike stopped the car at the end of the

road. He pointed to a faded wooden sign nailed to a large tree trunk. "The house is supposedly that way."

We hopped out of the car and trekked toward the house, using the lantern function on our phones to illuminate the way. I went ahead, avoiding talking to them. Not that they would talk to me, not when they were whispering about me behind my back.

"She's crazy."

"Is she that desperate for money?"

"I heard her aunt is crazy. I think she is too."

"Did you know she's not going to college? She's going to stay in this hellhole. I almost pity her."

I sped up, trying to put some distance between them and me, so I didn't have to listen to their mean words. One thing my aunt had drilled into me was respect. Even when you didn't particularly like someone or have anything in common with them, you showed them respect.

I guess their parents hadn't taught them that.

Blinded by my rage and stupidity—seriously, why the hell had I volunteered to do this?—I only saw the house once I was practically at its doorstep. My stomach dropped as I lifted my head and took it in. The house was three stories tall, with a round turret on the right, a wraparound porch, and a balcony on the second floor. The wooden walls were rotten, the windows and doors broken, the roof either missing or caved in, and the grass around it overgrown.

As if teasing me, a chilly breeze brushed past me, sending a shiver down my spine.

"Now, that is one haunted house," Noah said from right behind me.

"You could say that again," Karla muttered.

Mike walked to me. "All right, Erin. See here?" He flashed

the money in front of my face. "Fifteen hundred dollars. It'll all be yours if you stay inside the house for an hour."

Shit. So much for easy money.

I looked at each of them. They had gone to high school like normal kids, and now they all would be leaving our shitty town to go to college and pursue their dreams. They all also had way more money than me.

A part of me resented them for having more opportunities at their feet.

Another part of me was disgusted that I had come so low.

Too late to back up now.

"Just sit tight," I said, forcing my voice to sound normal, even. "See you in an hour."

Holding my breath, I walked forward. I forced my feet to keep moving at a steady pace, even when I stepped onto the porch and it creaked beneath my feet. Even when I pushed open the front door and almost fell back. Even when I entered the house and the light from my phone didn't seem like enough.

I halted in the foyer, trying to find my bearings before picking a spot to sit down and wait. Wide, curving stairs hugged the wall on the other side of the broken chandelier lying in the middle of the foyer, and an archway opened underneath the stairs.

"Go farther inside!" Mike yelled from outside.

Groaning, I closed my eyes for a moment and thought about the money. Money. Money. Money. It was the only reason I was doing this, right?

It had been stupid, really. I had been alone at the town square, contemplating how I would go home and show my aunt the stack of college applications I had gathered. Although I had been homeschooled all my life, I knew all the kids and teenagers in town. When Mike and his gang walked past me, talking about their bright futures and the many colleges that had accepted them, I felt angry. Jealous. Why could they go, and I couldn't? Because we didn't have money? Because I would have to move away? Those didn't seem like plausible excuses, even if my aunt was a freaking general and expected me to obey her every wish.

I had thought about running away several times, to live my own life and go to college and do whatever pleased me, but I knew my aunt would just go after me and either drag me back or come with me. To her, I would always be a little girl.

Then, these dumbasses had to talk about a dare. When Mike kept raising the bid for whoever went in the haunted house and none of them manned up, I volunteered.

I guess the biggest dumbass here was me.

Inhaling deeply, I opened my eyes and walked beyond the foyer.

I crossed under the archway and found myself in a living room. Spiderwebs dangled from the high ceiling, and a few furniture items were covered by white sheets and dust. I put a hand over my nose, trying to cover the moldy scent emanating from the house, and breathed through my mouth.

To my left, double doors, mostly off their hinges, opened to another room with built-in shelves that extended to the ceiling. It probably was a library once. To my right was another large room, which resembled a dining room, and beyond it the kitchen. The cabinet doors twisted on their hinges, and the appliances were missing, but it was easy to see this house was old—probably from a time when refrigerators hadn't been invented yet.

Despite the look and odor, this place wasn't bad. We all

had heard about the haunted house just outside Spring Hill. I just never thought much about it. Who knew it wasn't haunted at all, just old and uncared for?

Still, being alone in this house made me uneasy.

I went back to the living room and looked around, trying to find a spot without a lot of dust so I could sit down. Something shiny flashed to my right. I looked in its direction. There was something underneath the couch.

But I wasn't here to find things. All I needed to do was sit down and wait. But as I turned my back, the shiny object underneath the couch seemed to shine brighter.

"What the hell …?"

Curious, I crouched down beside the sheet-covered couch and reached for the item. I picked it up and stood, my eyes on the strange item. It was a gold chain, with a pendant—thin metal twisted around a deep red stone. In my hand, it didn't seem to shine as much, but it was still pretty.

Very, very pretty.

I glanced around the house. This necklace might have been here for years. If I took it, nobody would notice, right? I shook my head. What the hell was I thinking? Even if this jewelry was beautiful and expensive and ownerless, I couldn't take it. It wasn't right.

Yet, I didn't want to drop it.

I couldn't.

I put my phone down on the couch's armrest, opened the chain, and hooked it around my neck.

An electric jolt coursed through me, making me gasp and almost driving me to my knees.

What the hell was that?

I reached for the chain's clasp, eager to take off the necklace, but I couldn't. The clasp wouldn't open. Seriously? I didn't want this damn necklace. I tugged on it, hoping it was so old that the chain would snap, but I only ended up cutting the skin on the back of my neck.

A moment later, a scream pierced the quiet.

My blood chilled.

"Erin, get out!" someone yelled from the outside.

I ran to the foyer, but the door shut in my face. Panic started in my stomach and spread as I grabbed the knob and tried to open the freaking door, to no avail.

"This is not funny!" I banged on the door. "Let me out!" Another scream echoed from outside, then it all went quiet. "Guys? You're there, right? Open the door!"

Nobody answered.

I leaned my back against the locked door and inhaled deeply, trying to calm my nerves and think. This was a mean prank. Mike and the others had planned all of this from the beginning, I was sure. Why, I had no idea. I had never done anything to them. Regardless, they were having way too much fun at my expense. Screaming and locking the door to scare me? That was a low blow.

I would climb out a broken window and kick their damn asses from here to hell.

My heart beating so fast that it hurt, I ran back to the living room, past the couches, and to one of the French doors in the back.

I was a few feet from it when dark shadows appeared behind the glass doors.

My knees trembled.

The waist-high, gray-skinned monster hopped into the living room. They bared their pointy teeth and stared at me with their yellow cat-like eyes, as they dragged their large feet toward me.

"Stay back!" I cried, retreating a few steps.

But I halted, as soon as I realized there were more of them —coming from the kitchen, the library, the balcony from upstairs, the foyer ... They had me surrounded.

I put my fingers to my temple and closed my eyes.

"This isn't real. This isn't real," I repeated to myself.

But when I opened my eyes, the little monsters were even closer.

"Give it to us," one of them said, his voice chilling, his words slurring.

Give what?

The necklace. I reached for it, but it wouldn't open. It was stuck around my neck.

"I can't—"

One of the little monsters jumped over me, his hands clawing at the pendant. Screaming, I fell on my butt. I tried pushing the monster back, but another one pulled my hair, while another tugged at my blouse, and another grabbed my shoe.

Holy shit, holy shit, holy shit. This couldn't be real.

I screamed. I swatted my arms and kicked my feet, trying to get rid of them.

It couldn't be real. Monsters and ghosts didn't exist.

A little creature tugged on the necklace, hurting my neck. I screamed, thinking he would decapitate me if he tugged any harder. I lifted my arm, pushing the monster back, but not before it scratched my forearm with its long, clawlike fingers.

Another one snatched the necklace and pulled harder. The chain broke, hurting me, scratching my skin. The little creature cradled the necklace, then dashed away. But the others advanced on me.

"Erin!"

My breath caught.

I knew that voice.

"Aunt Paula! I'm here," I yelled. I looked up at the second-floor landing.

My aunt stood on the ledge, where the rail had been broken and was now missing, her hair pulled up into a ponytail, wearing dark leather clothing and holding a sword with a dark blade.

She jumped over the balcony, landing effortlessly a few feet from me. With a murderous glint in her hazel eyes, she swung her sword wide, cutting through three of the little monsters.

Their bodies fell on the ground right beside me.

Then, the other monsters jumped on her.

I stared in awe as Aunt Paula moved like a ninja. She spun out of reach, stabbed and slashed, as if she had been fighting all her life. The awe turned into wariness. Who was she? How did she know how to fight like that? Why didn't she ever tell me?

Aunt Paula lifted her sword above her head. A dark glow emanated from the blade and the remaining little monsters cowered. She turned to me and grabbed my hand. "Listen to me," she said, her eyes wide, her voice absolute. "You have to run. Get out of here and run. Go back to our house and stay there."

"W-what?" I held her hand. "What about you?"

"I'll stop them, then I'll join you."

I shook my head. "I don't like this."

She offered me a forced smile. "It's okay. I'll be okay." She freed herself from me. "Now go."

I didn't want to leave her alone in this damned house, but she seemed to know what she was doing. I nodded, then turned to run back into the foyer. I took two steps before I skidded to a halt.

A bigger, wider shadow fell in my way.

A monster at least five times the height of the little ones stepped forward. Dressed all in black and with fair skin and black hair, the monster looked almost human. Almost. His eyes were all black, his ears were pointy, his teeth were razor-sharp. A low growl came from his throat. Fear paralyzed me. I tried moving, running, screaming, but found myself frozen.

The monster lifted his big, lean, sharp hand.

"Erin, no!"

My aunt pushed me out of the way.

The monster dropped his claws.

My aunt's body fell to the floor.

2

"I NEED MORE TIME," THE MAN BEGGED.

I had been doing this for almost a thousand years, and it was always the same. A stupid person sold their soul to a higher demon in exchange for something. When their time was up, the person cried for more time.

Typical fucking human behavior.

Bored, I glanced at the time on my cell phone. "The date and time in your contract are coming up in two minutes."

Hands pressed together, the man knelt on the floor. "Please, please. I can't leave yet. My family depends on me."

Oh, I knew that well. After working part-time at the local daycare, the man's wife was home waiting for their twins to get home from school. He was at his shitty little office, working extra hours to make ends meet. If only he had been smarter about making a demonic contract.

"One minute," I warned him.

"No, no." Tears welled in his eyes.

Ten years ago, the man's wife, who couldn't have kids, found out she had cancer. By luck—or bad luck—the man stumbled onto me. Doing my job, I offered him a contract: His wife would be cured of cancer and able to have kids. But after ten years, his soul would belong to my boss in the underworld.

The time had come. The man's wife had been cured and they had children, but their financial status had worsened. In a few seconds, the man would be gone and his family would be left to rot.

Like I said, the man should have been smarter.

A terrible thing to say, but business was fucking business.

I sighed. "Time is up." His small office darkened, and shadows appeared in the corners. Eyes wide, the man trembled from head to toe as the shadows took form—bodies of humans, with long limbs and sharp claws. "Get him," I told the shadows.

The man screamed.

I walked out of his office, closing the door behind me. Even though the shadows were ripping his soul to pieces right now and he was screaming his lungs out, nobody could hear him. In a few minutes, the people I walked past as I left the building wouldn't even remember seeing me. In a while, they would find his lifeless body on the floor.

On the street, I flicked the contract and it disappeared. "One down, three zillions more to go."

In my thousand years working for the higher demon Asmodeus, I had done many odd jobs, but the one he enjoyed the most was the writing of contracts—and the collecting of souls.

I went around finding desperate people and getting them to sign away their souls. The time left they had depended on what they asked for. The bigger the wish, the less time they got.

Unlike me.

Almost a thousand years ago, I had sold my soul to Asmodeus, a prince of the underworld. I had been young, only twenty-two years old, and stupid and immature. All I wanted was to save my mother and sister from the plague consuming our village. I hadn't realized until it was too late that Asmodeus had tricked me. Instead of giving me a time-frame like he did everyone, my contract was for eternity.

I had to work for the higher demon and do his bidding until the end of time.

Per my schedule, I secured three more contracts before heading to the Dark Creek Pub, a local bar in Liberty Creek. I paused before the door and fixed my black suit. There was sure to be nagging inside, and the fewer reasons I gave him to find something wrong, the better.

After a long breath, I went into the bar.

As usual, Asmodeus sat at a booth in the corner, drinking his whiskey on the rocks. I didn't fear much, but every time I saw him, it struck me how powerful Asmodeus was, how intimidating.

He could destroy half of the country with a snap of his fingers.

He could infuse excruciating pain in my body with just a look.

A look similar to the one he was giving me right now—his blue eyes narrowed, his thick brows slightly curled down, his jaw set. The only thing that was always the same was his long blond hair. Unmoving and shiny. I had heard female demons longed for a hair like his. While I had heard from male demons that they wished they looked as regal and young as him—Asmodeus's human form appeared to be in his late twenties, but his true age was unknown. But from the information I gathered over the years, I knew he was at least five thousand years old.

I took a seat across the table and placed the stack of contracts in front of him.

Asmodeus lowered his gaze to the folders and counted them. "Well done." He flicked his hand once. The contracts vanished and a glass of whiskey appeared in front of me.

"Thanks," I muttered, reaching for the drink. I was more of an ice-cold beer kind of guy, but I wouldn't argue with him about such small matters. "I should be able to collect three more contracts tonight."

The high demon waved his hand. "I have another task for you. Let's call it a special mission."

I frowned. Usually, I hated the special missions he sent me on. "What is it?"

"A new semester is about to start at the Blackthorn Hunters Academy. You'll go back there, pretend to be a student and Randall's little puppy ..." He leaned forward, his elbows on the table. "And you're going to kill him."

"But ..." I pressed my lips tight, measuring my words. Despite what I said and what argument I brought up, I saw no way out of this. "That's impossible." Randall was the first demon hunter and the headmaster of the Blackthorn Hunters Academy. He was immortal, incredibly powerful, and practically impossible to kill. "Haven't you tried before? You're much stronger than I am."

Asmodeus face hardened. "I could have killed him, but other circumstances arose and I had to give up." He brought his glass to his lips and drank the contents in one long swallow. "This time, we need to kill him."

"May I ask why?" I dared to ask, though I braced myself.

Surprisingly, he didn't hesitate before answering. "I want

to take over the academy. We'll kill the demon hunters before they finish their training, so that our demons can come out of the underworld. They will be unhindered and can take over the world." A sly grin appeared on his lips. "We'll be the most powerful demons ever."

I shook my head. "I can see the appeal—"

"Randall trusts you," Asmodeus said, his voice eager, excited, as if this was already a done deal. "You can approach him without any suspicion and kill the bastard."

"It's not that easy." Had I mentioned the hunter was immortal and fucking powerful?

"I'm willing to offer you payment for this job," Asmodeus said.

I scoffed. He had offered me incentives before. What would it be this time? Money, more power, women. "Such as?"

"Your freedom."

My body went rigid. My breath caught. "W-what?"

"Kill Randall and I'll destroy your contract and give you your soul back."

My soul. My freedom.

I would once more be the owner of my fucking life.

This was way too tempting.

"What's the catch?" I asked, sure he was hiding a card up his sleeve.

"No catch. Kill Randall before the end of the semester, and I'll give you your soul back. Simple as that." Asmodeus extended his hand to me. "Do we have a deal, my son?"

I hesitated, but I didn't care about Randall. If killing him gave me back my wretched life, I would do it.

I slipped my hand into Asmodeus's. "Yes, Father."

* * *

WHEN I FIRST MET ASMODEUS, I HAD NO IDEA WHO HE WAS. But he knew who I was. He knew he was my father. He told me I was a half-demon and that he wanted to take me to the underworld with him, but I refused. Then my mother and sister got sick and were dying. He came back saying he would save them if I sold my soul to him.

I didn't think twice.

Because he was a higher demon, a prince of the underworld, he had given me a special place beside him. At first, I had rebelled, but after about three hundred years, I didn't care anymore. It all became automatic—do whatever he told me, endure the underworld, command legions of demons.

It was like breathing now.

When I left the bar, the sun was almost set and nighttime was near. As I walked to my car, parked in the main square, one of the many shadows hiding in town approached me. It told me where to find a lesser demon who owed Asmodeus a favor and who had been hiding from us for a couple of months. If I went after him right now and made him pay before I headed back to the academy, Asmodeus would be satisfied.

So, I followed the shadow's lead.

I took my car out of town, to the parking lot of a hiking trail. I left my car there, and walked down the trail the shadow mentioned, my demon eyes adjusting to the darkening skies. Then, I steered away from it, going toward the base of the mountain.

The demon was supposed to have a hideout around here, a cave where he lured clueless humans hiking the trails, and finished them. After looking for a few minutes, I found the cave, but besides some furniture, clothes, jewelry, books, and liquor bottles, there was nothing there. The demon wasn't here.

I stepped out of the cave and extended my senses. Asmodeus had made me powerful, but I was still only half-demon, and my senses didn't work the same way his did.

I couldn't sense the damn demon, but I felt another disturbance in the air, somewhere to my right. I frowned in that direction. One human thing Asmodeus had worked to erase was my curiosity. Unfortunately, that hadn't worked well, though I was able to suppress it for the most part. Why should I bother suppressing it? The semester at the academy started tomorrow, and I would be back among humans. I could afford wasting a little bit more time.

Following my curiosity, I went to the right, to the south. I only had to walk a few minutes before I stood in front of a ramshackle old house.

I had heard of this house. It was said to be haunted, though I had never bothered to check it out. I could feel a faint hint of disturbance coming from it. Perhaps it was fucking haunted.

Haunted houses didn't concern me, so I walked away.

I had taken three steps when a scream pierced the quiet of the mountain.

Without thinking, I ran toward the house.

3

ERIN

I stared at my aunt's body on the floor. Her open, wide eyes stared up. Her chest didn't move. My brain didn't register those details as I crawled to her, and shook her shoulder.

"Aunt Paula," I said, my voice breaking. "Get up!"

Her head lolled to the side.

A scream ripped from my throat and I scooted back.

No, no, no.

A hair-raising growl boomed through the living room. My blood chilled. The monster. I had forgotten about him.

I turned and stood as the monster charged at me. I clambered back, my feet tripping on the dark sword. My aunt's sword. Hands trembling, I grabbed the weapon and pointed at the monster.

"Don't come any closer!" I yelled, my voice high-pitched.

The monster let out something that resembled laughter but sounded more like a moan. "What are you going to do, little girl?"

I frowned. Little girl, me? I wasn't the tallest girl out there, but I sure wasn't little.

"I'll rip you to pieces," I said, though I was sure that if he advanced another step and swung his long arm, he would not only knock the sword out of my hand, but knock me over too.

A hissing sound came from behind me. Shit, I had forgotten about the little creatures. I glanced over my shoulder to the advancing nasty monsters. Once more, I was surrounded, but this time, a big creature was ready to eat me alive.

This time, I didn't have my aunt to save me.

I jutted the sword out again. "I'm warning you."

As if mocking me, the demon advanced much faster than I thought he could move. He wrapped his long fingers around my wrist and tugged me to him. "I'm not going to kill you," the monster said.

Did he think I would buy that? I tried jerking away, but he was much stronger than I could ever dream of being. He leaned forward and kissed my wrist.

Disgust knotted in my stomach.

The monster let me go.

I stumbled back, almost falling over the little creatures.

A sharp-toothed smile took over the monster's face, his mouth wide, terrifying. "Now, you're marked."

I blinked at him. What?

It didn't matter. I gripped the sword tighter. "Go to hell!" I lunged at him before he made a move at me.

The monster flicked his wrist. A punch-like pressure hit my chest and I fell back, falling on my butt and losing my grip on the sword.

With his wicked grin, the monster leaned over me.

Fear choked my throat and shook my limbs.

This was it. This was when and where I died.

And no one would care or know.

Defeated, I closed my eyes.

"Hey, you big, ugly demon!"

My breath caught at the new voice. Opening my eyes, I searched for the owner, but didn't see anyone right away. All I saw was the big monster turning around, facing whoever had called him.

Then, the little monsters jumped on me.

I screamed.

For a full ten seconds, panic paralyzed me. But then I tried reining it in. I slapped the little creatures, trying to move them away from me, then reached for where I had dropped the sword.

My fingers brushed against the cold blade at the same time a little creature bit my shoulder. I screamed. I reached forward, closed my hand around the hilt of the sword, and then brought it over my shoulder, cutting the back of the little monster.

He fell to the floor with a dull thud. A moment later, his body shimmered, turning into a pool of green goo.

My stomach turned, and I thought I would lose my lunch.

I didn't have a moment to breathe. The other little creatures came at me. Not sure what I was doing, I swung the sword to one side and the other, trying to hit them, or at least to keep them away.

I killed a few of them. Their bodies turned into the same green goo from before, creating a pool around me.

Then, one little monster bit my forearm and I dropped the sword. Another one of them kicked it away.

"What the ...?"

The little creatures swarmed me.

A heavy thud shook the house walls and the little ones froze.

Beside us, the bigger beast lay flat in the green goo on the floor, his head a few feet away.

My stomach turned.

"Are you okay?"

I forced my focus away from the gore and disgust, and looked up. Behind the corpse, a man stood, holding a sword similar to my aunt's.

"I ..." I didn't know what to say.

Twirling his sword, the man advanced on the little minions. Shrieking, they ran.

The man lowered his sword and approached me. He stared at me. "Are you okay?"

I opened my mouth to say yes, but I couldn't. It wasn't true. I couldn't process this, but one thing was for sure: I wasn't okay. "No," I muttered.

Here in the dark, I couldn't see much of his features, but I knew his gaze had fallen to the sword a few feet from us. With a sigh, he grabbed my wrist. "First, let's get you out of here."

With no strength left in me, I let him guide me to the foyer, then to the front porch, where he pushed me down to sit on the steps.

Outside, the moon shone high, giving a faint brilliance to the world below. I could almost make out the shape of the trees surrounding the house, the broken porch rails, the stains on the wooden floor.

And how Mike, Karla, Jennifer, Noah, Justin, and Alisha were nowhere to be found. Had the monsters eaten them? Or had they gotten away when I first screamed? Though I hated them for leaving me alone here, I chose to believe they were safe now.

Sword gone, the man placed my phone, still with the

lantern function on, beside me. He took a couple of steps back and stared at me. "Who's the hunter?"

I frowned. "Hunter?"

"The woman inside the house."

"M-my aunt."

"We shouldn't leave her body like that," he said, his tone firm, cold. "Do you have any family you can call to come take her?"

I shook my head. "There's no one else," I muttered. Holy shit, my aunt was gone. She was gone and I was alone.

The man tsked. "If you're not against it, I'll find a nice spot close by and bury her."

Bury her? Wait ... I could barely process the fact that she was dead, and this stranger was talking about burying her? He continued, "Do you have any other ideas? Take her body into town and give her a proper burial? Wouldn't that make things even more difficult?"

Shit, he was right. How could I take her into town and explain what happened? Not even I understood what had happened.

But the thought of burying my aunt ... my stomach turned once more.

Pushing the uneasy away, I stood. "I want to help."

The man pressed his lips. "I'm not sure that's a good idea."

"She's my aunt. Was," I corrected myself, the word catching in my throat. Oh, shit, this reality hurt more with each passing second. "If you're going to bury her, I want to help you."

"Fine," he snapped.

In the end, the man did almost everything alone. I grabbed her sword from the floor, while the man found a good place beside a stream, dug most of the hole alone, carried my aunt's body by himself, and buried her while I turned away and threw up.

This couldn't be freaking happening.

It couldn't.

If I hadn't opened my mouth, if I hadn't pitched my crazy idea to Mike and the others, if I hadn't entered the house alone, my aunt wouldn't have come and she wouldn't be dead right now.

Because of me, my aunt was dead.

We might not have had the best relationship, but she was still the only family I had left.

Nauseous again, I dry-heaved against a tree, hidden from the man who was now closing my aunt's grave.

There were more crazy things to consider. Unreal things. Monsters? Magical swords?

"I know you must have lots of questions," the man said. He appeared on the other side of the tree, his hands clean, despite the fact that I was sure I had seen him burying them in the dirt a few moments ago. "Why don't you come with me? We can go back into town, where you might feel safer, and I'll explain everything to you."

Go somewhere with this stranger. Well, he had saved me from the monsters, he had buried my aunt when I couldn't, and he was offering to tell me more about the craziness swimming in my mind. If he wanted to harm me, he would have done it already. Actually, he would have watched while the monsters ate me alive.

Besides, where else could I go now? Back home, where my aunt wasn't waiting for me? To that shitty town where I had lived most of my life and still barely knew my own neighbors?

Not caring about right or wrong, I nodded. "All right."

* * *

I DIDN'T REMEMBER MUCH OF THE WALK TO THE MAN'S CAR, OR where it had been parked. Or when he gave me healing cream to apply to the bites on my shoulders and arms, or when he gave me a spare jacket to put on. Or when he drove into Liberty Creek and stopped the car in front of a rundown diner at the edge of town. Or even when we walked in the diner and took a booth in the corner.

I finally woke up once the waitress brought the menus to us and the strong scent of cigarette and cinnamon emanating from her filled my nostrils, bringing forth the nauseous feeling.

"All right," the man said, taking one of the menus. "I think we could start with our names. I'm Rey Lowe."

Right. I focused on the conversation so I wouldn't throw up again. "Erin Delman."

"How old are you?"

"Just turned nineteen."

"What about the woman who was with you?"

An image of her still body on the floor of the haunted house flashed in my mind. Suddenly, all the other scents of the diner became too strong—apple pie, fries, pancakes with syrup, coffee, chocolate milkshakes.

I pressed a hand over my stomach, willing it to stop turning. "My aunt, Paula."

"From what I could gather, you didn't know she was a demon hunter?"

"A what?" Was I hearing him right, or was I still too numb to understand anything? Or perhaps this had all been a dream, a nightmare. I had to pinch myself and wake up. I reached for my arm.

Rey gently slapped my hand away. "You're not dreaming."

A hollow chuckle bubbled out of my mouth. "It's the only way I can explain everything that is happening."

"No. I can explain what is happening," Rey said.

Before, in the house, the hiking trail, and in the car, it had been too hard to make out his features, but now, seated in the diner, the dim light was enough. For the first time, I actually looked at him. He didn't look that much older than me, maybe twenty-one or twenty-two. He had a mop full of dirty blond hair framing his sharp-cut, clean-shaven face. His skin was fair and his eyes were a shiny gray that reminded me of a cool rainy day. He had seemed tall when walking by my side, and now I could see his wide shoulders and slim arms under the black suit. Wait, black suit? Who went hiking in a suit?

I frowned. "What were you doing in the mountains? How did you find me?"

"I was nearby on business," Rey said, his voice deep. "I heard you screaming and went to help. I had no idea I would find another demon hunter in that house."

What the hell ...? "You keep saying that."

"What? Demon hunter."

"Yes. I don't even know what that means."

"I can ..." His voice faded when the waitress approached.

"Are you ready to order?" she asked in her sugar-coated voice. Whatever mint she had to disguise the scent of the cigarette wasn't helping.

My stomach was too upset to think about food, but Rey ordered food for us anyway.

Once the waitress was gone, I started, "Please, tell me

something that makes sense, because honestly, what I just witnessed ... it can't be real."

"I'm sorry to say it was all real," Rey said. "Demon hunters are a type of supernatural with special abilities. They protect humans against the demons who come from the underworld and torment humans and their world." He paused. "Your aunt was a demon hunter."

I shook my head. "She would have told me."

"Erin, I won't pretend to know why she didn't tell you, but there's one more thing you should know. That sword she had, the sword you used to kill the little imps? It has a name. It's called a Dawnblade and it can only be wielded by demon hunters."

I frowned at him, not sure what he was trying to say. Then, it dawned on me. "No. No. Not me. I would have known."

"If you had been raised in our world, maybe, but I believe your aunt, Paula, was trying to hide this world from you. If you noticed your increased strength or agility, she probably chalked it up that you were talented, or whatever."

I gaped at him.

There had been a few situations when I did notice I was a little stronger than other people, a little more agile, sometimes a lot faster. When I asked my aunt about it, she said I was different, like how some athletes seemed to be able to do the impossible—she said I had many useless talents.

"But why?" I whispered.

"I don't know," Rey said. "What I do know is that your aunt is gone and you're all alone." He reached across the table, grabbed my hand, and turned my arm so that the inside of my wrist was up. There was a dark, swirly mark where the monster had kissed me. "This is a demon's kiss.

That particular demon branded you, so he can later have your soul for himself in the underworld." I gasped. "I killed him, but the mark will draw other demons in."

I rubbed at the mark. "How can I get it off?"

"It'll fade with time, but only if you stay alive. The only place safe for you now is the place where you'll be protected by other demon hunters and learn how to fight back."

I stared at him. "And where's that?"

"The Blackthorn Hunters Academy," he said, as if it was the most normal place in the world. "It's where demon hunters are trained. It's where you could learn about your abilities and use them."

I didn't care about any of that. Why would I? Until this morning, supernaturals and magic and demons didn't exist. Until this morning, I was complaining that the hardest part of my life was not being able to attend college. Until this morning, my aunt was alive.

This was too much.

I shook my head. "I don't want to go anywhere."

"Then where you'll go? How will you keep yourself safe?"

I'll I looked down at the menu for a moment. The only option I saw was going back to my house. How would I live there without my aunt? How would I explain her absence? Where would I work and make a living?

How would I fight off the demons that came for me? I didn't want to believe Rey. It didn't make sense that demons would want me. My brain still stumbled past believing demons were real, despite having been attacked by them.

Before I could come up with an answer, the waitress came back with our food. "Here you go, dears." She placed two plates with huge burgers and fries in front of us, followed by a coffee pot and two mugs. "Enjoy."

She walked away and I stared at the food.

"You seemed out of it, so I ordered what I was having for you," Rey said. "I hope it's okay."

"Yeah, it's fine." I turned the plate around, so the fries were closer. My stomach still didn't feel too good, but I knew I needed something. I would munch on the fries and drink the coffee, but I didn't think I could handle the burger right now.

"You didn't answer my question," Rey pressed. "How will you keep yourself safe?"

"What do you care?" I snapped. Rey's eyes widened. I let out a sigh. "Sorry. It's just …" I rubbed my fingertips on my temples. I felt a headache coming. "This is too much to take in."

"I understand." He nodded. "I really do. Unfortunately, I don't think you have much time. The demons will come soon. Besides, I'm going there tonight. To the academy. You can come with me."

Right. He had a sword like my aunt's with him. "You're a demon hunter."

"I am a student at the academy. Fourth and final year. Then, I'll become a demon hunter."

"Tell me, what is this academy like?"

One corner of his lips tugged up. "It's a great place, with fun classes, and lots of people our age. More importantly, they can offer you something you won't learn anywhere else: You'll learn to fight demons and defend yourself."

I let out a long sigh before sipping from my coffee. I needed more time to process all of this before deciding. Even if I had wanted to leave my previous life and run away and do something for myself, I had never imagined it could be something as crazy as this. I wasn't sure I was ready for all of this.

"I need more time," I muttered.

"Well, you have until I finish eating my burger." He picked up the burger. Until then, he had been eating only the fries. "After that, I'm leaving."

Shit.

My mind hurt from trying to assimilate all of this.

What would I do if I stayed? I didn't know. Sell the house? Go to college?

What if demons came for me, like Rey said they would? Then, I would end up dead, because I doubted I would be lucky to have someone like him saving me a second time.

But what if I went with him? I had always liked paranormal books and movies, and I often thought of how cool it would be to have superpowers. Here was Rey telling me demons and supernaturals existed and that I had powers, even if I didn't feel them.

Even living with my aunt, I had always felt alone, as if something was missing from my life. Honestly, there had been so much—warmth, purpose, friends.

I was now being presented with the opportunity to belong somewhere, to go to a special school and make friends, to learn a cool ability and rock it. I imagined myself like Selene from Underworld—holy shit, that would just be crazy awesome.

To be honest, I didn't have a choice here. Either I stayed and died, or I went with this stranger to the academy.

Rey was halfway done with his burger, but there was no reason to wait to tell him my answer. I inhaled deeply and said, "All right. I'll go to the academy with you."

4

I didn't know why I was helping this girl. She was nothing to me. I had just met her.

Typically, I would have ignored the screams, or helped and then walked away. I didn't help humans often, but I felt like with all the fucked up things I had done for my father, I should at least try to atone for some of it.

But there was something about this girl. One, I hadn't expected to see her holding a Dawnblade. Only a demon hunter could hold those specially crafted swords. And two, she was fucking pretty. That sounded silly, but it was true. I had been alive for a long time and seen millions of women, lain with several too, and even though I was sure Erin's beauty wasn't uncommon, there was something about her that made me want to stare at her and take in every inch of her delicate face, carving it into memory.

Eyes fixed on the wall beside us, Erin popped another french fry into her mouth. Her long black hair needed a good brush, her clothes were dirty under my big jacket, but she still looked beautiful with her fair skin, her brilliant and unusual golden eyes, and her pink lips. There were a few freckles across her thin nose, and I could see a pair of dimples forming on her cheeks when she chewed.

And even with all the perspiration from the fright and the dirt from the blood and the dusty house, I could still make out her sweet rose scent. It was like a beacon, luring me to her.

Why did I feel so drawn to her?

My phone rang. I picked it up and glanced at the screen.

"Hey, Wyatt," I answered. Erin turned her golden eyes to me, but quickly lowered her gaze to the coffee mug.

"Hey, man," Wyatt said. "Where are you?"

"I'm at a diner right now."

"At Big Red's?"

"That one."

"I'm half a block away," Wyatt said. "I'll meet you there."

"But—"

He turned off the call before I could warn him I was leaving soon.

"Everything okay?" Erin asked, her voice low. It was obvious she was still out of it, still not processing things right. I couldn't blame her. She had lost her aunt and found out demons were real and trying to dominate the world.

Plus, she was a demon hunter; I was sure of it.

I felt a little icky about pushing her to go to the academy, but it was the only safe place for her right now. Even with Asmodeus's plans to kill Randall and take over the academy and kill all the demon hunters. Honestly, I didn't think I would be able to kill Randall anytime soon. Until then, it was better for her to stay at the academy.

"Yeah, everything is fine." I pocketed my phone. "Are you ready?"

Erin hesitated but nodded.

After I stopped by the counter to pay the bill, Erin and I walked out to the street. That was when I realized she didn't have anything on her other than her phone. No purse, no documents, no money, no extra clothes. Perhaps before going to the academy, we should swing by her place and get some of her things.

"There you are," Wyatt said. I turned toward his voice and found him a few feet from us.

Wyatt was a werewolf without a pack. He had moved to Colorado a few months ago to hide from his past, though he never elaborated on it. All I knew was that he drank too much, and with his hot wolf temper, he was always up for a fight.

I had saved Wyatt's life from a bunch of demons, and since then, we had become good acquaintances. Mostly, we met at a bar occasionally and drank the night away.

"What's up?" I asked.

"I was going to invite you to go to the bar for a drink." His eyes shifted to the girl beside me. "But I see you have company."

"Erin, this is Wyatt," I said, gesturing from her to him. She extended her hand to him. "He's a werewolf." She pulled back her hand. I chuckled. "It's okay. Wyatt is a good werewolf."

She frowned and muttered, "Are there such things as good werewolves?"

"You're in for a surprise," I said, thinking about all she would learn about our world. "Wyatt, this is Erin. I think she's a demon hunter." Then, I whispered too low for human ears, "She's new to all this, so don't take it personally." Wyatt moved his chin a centimeter down, letting me know he had heard me with his super hearing.

"Hi, Erin," Wyatt said, his voice calm, leveled. So unlike him. "I understand your reservations. If I hadn't been born into this world, I would probably be skeptical too."

"It's too much to take in," Erin said. She still looked and sounded shocked.

"I understand." Wyatt frowned. "But I wanted to tell you one thing. Though demon hunters don't like werewolves, I hope you and I are an exception."

"Okay, man, don't overwhelm her." I glanced at Erin again. She was dirty and probably tired too. Taking her from here to the academy might be too much. An idea popped into my mind. "You know what? It's too late to go to the academy now. By the time we get there, it'll be the middle of the night and we won't be allowed inside."

Erin's delicate brows knotted. "What do you mean?"

"We should stay here tonight," I said. "Wyatt, think we can crash at your place?"

Wyatt's eyes widened. "Hm, my place is small and it's messy. But ... I know a place you can stay. Come with me."

* * *

WYATT TAGGED ALONG WITH ERIN AND ME, AND I DROVE US TO the place Wyatt had mentioned. It was a small apartment building. Before bidding us goodnight, Wyatt told me the owner of the apartment was a woman who had turned into a vampire and upped and left. So far, no one knew she was gone, but her family would probably come looking for her eventually.

But for now, it was a neat, clean place for Erin and me to spend the night.

"Call me if you need anything," Wyatt said, before leaving.

I didn't tell Erin whom the apartment belonged to or why it was empty. I let her believe it was owned by one of Wyatt's friends. She was out of town and he was housesitting for her.

There was only one bedroom and one bathroom in the apartment.

"You can take the bedroom," I told Erin. "I'll sleep on the couch."

She glanced at me, then the couch a few feet to the side. "You're too tall for the couch."

"I'll be okay." I gestured toward the bathroom. "You should take a shower and borrow some clothes."

Still moving in slow motion, Erin looked down at herself. My jacket could fit two of her inside, and her blouse was smeared with green and red blood—from the demons and her aunt. Her jeans didn't look much better either.

Erin took off my jacket. "You're right." She handed me the jacket before taking stiff steps into the bedroom. A moment later, she appeared again, carrying a change of clothes in her hands, then she stepped into the bathroom and closed the door.

With an exhale, I sat on the couch. I tried not to think about the beautiful girl undressing behind the flimsy door. Instead, I thought of all the things I should tell her to prepare her before she arrived at the academy.

I was ready for a long talk when she walked out of the bathroom twenty minutes later, with her hair wet and wearing loose sweatpants and a big T-shirt—apparently the owner of this apartment was also much taller than Erin.

However, Erin looked like a zombie on her feet.

She muttered, "Good night," before disappearing into the bedroom and closing the door.

All right. That was okay. She needed to rest. I could talk to her tomorrow while we drove the five hours to the academy.

I glanced at the couch and sighed. Erin had been right. It would be too small for me, so instead of trying to squeeze on it and wake up with my back hurting, I grabbed a pillow and a throw blanket and lay on the rug on the floor.

I closed my eyes, but my mind wouldn't shut up and my body was fucking restless. Still, I forced myself to stay still.

It seemed I had closed my eyes when I heard a soft noise, almost like a mouse hiding in the corner. I sat up and looked around, but there was no one, no mouse.

The sound came again. I used my half-demon senses to hear it better.

It was Erin, crying in the bedroom.

Before I could register what I was doing, I was on my feet and walking to the bedroom. I knocked on the door and opened it.

A table lamp illuminated a little of the room. Erin was on the bed, the covers bunched up around her bare legs, the big T-shirt barely covering her thighs.

I swallowed and forced my eyes to her face. "Erin, are you okay?"

Erin wiped the tears from her face and inhaled deeply, trying to calm down. "Honestly, I'm not sure." She let out a strangled chuckle. "I think I'm not okay."

I stepped into the room. "Want to talk about it?"

She shrugged. "Talking about it won't change what happened."

"No, but it might make your heart lighter." I cringed on the inside. What the fuck was I saying? Had I become a therapist now? Yet, I couldn't help myself. I sat down on the edge of the bed. "Why were you at that house?"

"It was so stupid." Tears welled in her eyes, giving them an even brighter golden shine. "It was a dare. Worst part is, I was the one who proposed it."

"You thought the house wasn't really haunted."

"Right. I never expected demons to be true. If I hadn't gone there, if I hadn't been so stupid ..."

She didn't finish her sentence, but I knew what she meant. If she hadn't gone in that house, her aunt would still be alive.

Something like sympathy swirled in my dead chest, bringing forth feelings I had thought I had forgotten. "I lost my mother and my sister too, long ago."

She wiped at her eyes, stopping the tears before they fell. "I'm so sorry."

I nodded. "I'll be honest, the pain will never go away. It'll only lessen a little, and you'll become stronger." I should know. I had been living with it for almost a thousand years. "Unfortunately, there's nothing left to do now but to move forward. Which is what you're doing by going to the academy with me."

Her brows curled down. "I know I agreed to go with you, but it still sounds like something unreal, like I'm dreaming, and soon I'll wake up in my bed and my aunt will come into my bedroom, bitching that I slept in."

"I wish it was a dream," I muttered. Despite this fucking feeling that pushed me to this girl, I wasn't entirely happy about her finding out and entering the supernatural world.

My world was ugly and deceiving. There were too many evil monsters, too many terrible battles, and even more unnecessary deaths.

But she had been kissed by a demon now. I couldn't just walk away, knowing that the moment I turned my back, the demons would come for her.

"Thanks," she whispered, her big eyes on mine.

I frowned. "What for?"

"Saving me. Bringing me with you. Taking me to this academy."

Fuck. With her looking at me like that, something else stirred in my chest.

I cleared my throat and stood up. "It's nothing. You should get some sleep now. Or at least try. We'll hit the road early."

"Okay," she said, her voice low.

I practically raced out of the bedroom and closed the door. Only then did I dare take a deep breath. My nose was nowhere like a vampire's, but it was much better than a human's, and while in the bedroom with Erin, her rose scent had teased me.

Everything about her messed me up.

What the fuck was going on? I had never been this affected by anyone before. This was ridiculous. I was just sympathizing with her over her loss and taking her to the academy because that was where I was headed.

No other reason.

Grunting under my breath, I lay down on the rug and forced myself to sleep.

* * *

"Thank you," Erin said, her mouth full with the big bite she took of the bagel I had given her. "I barely ate anything yesterday. My stomach was mad at me."

"No worries," I said, my eyes focused on the road.

Erin and I woke up early and hit the road, but before leaving town, I had stopped at a drive-thru and ordered some breakfast for us. It was a five-hour ride to the academy, and if I could avoid stopping on the way, I would.

Unless Erin told me she was hungry again. Then, we could stop.

What the fuck was I thinking? I shook my head and forced my mind to clear, to focus on the road.

After she was done with her bagel, Erin twisted her body to the side and faced me. "Tell me more about the academy, or about demons?"

"What do you want to know?"

"Anything. This is all new to me."

Glad to have something other than her alluring scent to focus on, I started. "Let's see. There are several rankings of demons. Lesser demons, neutral demons, higher demons, and grand demons. The lesser demons are the most common and numerous. Those imps that attacked you at the house were lesser demons. The bigger demon I fought was a neutral one. Don't let that term fool you. Neutral demons can be powerful." I paused. "Most higher demons and all grand demons can shapeshift into animals, and some of them can shapeshift into humans."

Erin frowned. "They must like that to trick the demon hunters."

I nodded. "They do, but with time, hunters developed ways to detect when a demon is shapeshifted. It isn't a hundred percent effective, but it works well most of the time."

Eyes still on me, Erin rested her head on the seat back and relaxed. "What else?"

It was hard to focus on the road, on the subject we were

talking about, when she looked at me like that. I cleared my throat and went on, "The other thing you should know is that the headmaster of the Blackthorn Academy is Randall Boucher. He was the first demon hunter. His descendants inherited his power and became demon hunters. You're one of them."

"You mean, we're all related?"

"In a way," I admitted. "But you have to understand that Randall is old. Like several millennia old, so the bloodlines have spread out a lot."

She gaped. "How is that possible?"

"Good question," I answered. "Nobody really knows how old he is, and how he managed to stay alive for so long. He's also the founder of the academy, which has been around for two thousand years." He was much older than that, though. Randall first created the Blackthorn hunters, a group of specialized demons hunters. However, with time, the number of hunters increased, and Randall decided to create the academy to prepare hunters before they joined the fight— and also to filter out hunters who might not be good at their work.

"Wow, I feel like he might be a celebrity."

"In a way, he is. He's powerful, the most powerful of all of us." And that was why my mission was so fucked up. If I ever was able to kill Randall, then that meant suicide too. There was no way I could kill him without using all my power.

"What else?" she urged.

I thought for a minute. What else would she, a young woman who had been living as a regular human, want to know? "Let's see. The academy is four years, and usually the students start at eighteen or nineteen and finish when they are twenty-two years old. It's a boarding school, so students stay in the dormitories, but most go home during winter break and summer vacation." I frowned. "Oh, and cell phones aren't allowed."

"What?" she practically shrieked.

"Yeah, I know. Everyone protests, but the headmaster won't change that rule. You can have it in your dorm room, but you can't carry it on campus. Also, no mention of the school or pictures of the school on social media."

"Social media makes sense," she muttered.

"Other than that, it's like a normal school. Classes all day, meals in the cafeteria, library open late for studying, special events here and there ... nothing much."

"Nothing much," she said with a snort. "For me, it's every-thing." She glanced out the window. "Everything is changing."

I understood, I really did, but I couldn't do much about that now.

The conversation died out. When I glanced to the side a few minutes later, Erin was sleeping. With her luscious hair falling to her waist, her face peaceful, her lashes touching her cheeks, she looked like an angel.

Once more, my feelings went too far before my mind could stop them. I felt sorry for her, but that was it. I couldn't get involved in her life. I would deliver her to the academy, and then I would wash my hands clean of her.

Erin slept the rest of the way.

I almost let her sleep until we were inside the academy, but I thought she would like to see it from the outside as we were arriving.

I gently touched her arm. "Erin, wake up."

She sat up, startled. Disoriented, she glanced around. "I fell asleep?"

I chuckled. "You did. But I thought you might want to be awake for this."

"For what?"

I turned the bend in the narrow road, and up ahead, tall, wrought iron gates appeared. "Welcome to the Blackthorn Hunters Academy."

5

ERIN

As we approached the gates, I couldn't believe my eyes.

The gates seemed tall from a distance, but when we got closer, I realized they were humongous. Black, wrought iron, with a crest in the center. Beside it, thick dark gray walls stretched into the distance. Black vines and thorns crept up the gates and walls, twisting around the iron bars, and over the top of the wall.

So far, the Blackthorn Hunters Academy looked powerful, dark, and eerie.

Rey slowed his car as the gates opened. I glanced out the passenger window, trying to see if there were any guards hidden behind the walls, but there was no one. I looked at Rey—there wasn't a remote control on the visor or in his hands. How did the gates open, then?

A corner of his lips curled up. "A lot of things that happen here will look impossible."

I was still not used to how deep and rough his voice was. Or how handsome he was. After the shock of my aunt's death, I hadn't processed more than his basic features, but now, I realized he was handsome. I usually didn't look twice at blond guys, but Rey might be the exception.

Focusing my attention back on the academy, I asked, "If it's not impossible, then how does it work?"

"Magic," he said. "It's all magic."

"Of course," I muttered.

Rey drove down a winding gravel road, flanked by beautiful and neatly manicured gardens, with tall trees, shrubs, and a few flowers.

The road opened up and the academy came into view. The main building, at the center, looked like a huge medieval castle. Vines and thorns climbed the gray walls and wrapped the narrow windows and the square towers. I could see other similar buildings.

Rey parked the car in an underground garage, and guided me up a narrow staircase, to the main building. We arrived in a big foyer of sorts, with double-, triple-high ceilings, and a heavy, dark metal chandelier with vines and thorns woven around It. The school crest overtook the entire back wall—an emblem with the letters BHA in the center, and thorny vines swirling around it.

Blackthorn Hunters Academy was the name of the school, and there were thorns everywhere. It seemed fitting.

A couple of students wearing white shirts and thin black jackets walked past us, their curious eyes on me. I managed to ignore them enough to take in their outfits. The girls wore black and green pleated skirts and black shoes, while the guys wore black slacks. So, I would be expected to wear something like that too?

"This is the Aster building," Rey said.

"Aster? Like the flower?"

"Yes. All buildings here have flower names." I wanted to

ask why but before I could he said, "This way." He directed me under an archway to a wide hallway with gray walls and black sconces that imitated old torches. The lightbulbs flickered like flames and dim electric light shone from them. "Up here." Rey gestured to the dark stone staircase to our right.

I had been so distracted taking it all in, I hadn't stopped to think where exactly he was taking me. "Where are we going?"

"We're almost there," he said, hurrying his steps down the hallway.

I frowned. So far, I had the impression that he hadn't minded my presence. After all, he had been the one who had saved me, taken me with him, and invited me to come with him to the academy. But now that we were here, he seemed eager to get rid of me.

Rey stopped in front of a black door and knocked on it. There was a silver plaque beside the door, but before I could read it, a voice from inside said, "Come in."

Rey opened the door and gestured for me to step inside the room.

Suddenly a little wary, I entered the room. It was a big office, with a black leather couch and glass coffee table to one side, and a long chestnut desk and leather chairs on the other. A woman with dark hair, dressed in a black suit with the school crest and a dark green shirt, stood behind the table.

Upon seeing me, her eyes widened, then narrowed. "Rey, what is the meaning of this?"

"Professor Martha, this is Erin Delman," he said. "I found her last night and I believe she's a demon hunter."

"How do you know?" Professor Martha asked, her voice hard.

"She wielded her aunt's Dawnblade."

"Where's her aunt now?"

"Dead."

Professor Martha took in a sharp inhale. "All right. Thank you, Rey. You may leave now."

Rey nodded once, then turned, and without looking at me, he left.

The moment the door closed behind him, I felt my world crash down. So this was it? He was abandoning me here? Maybe coming here wasn't my best decision.

"Professor—"

"Your aunt," Professor Martha started, cutting me off. "She was a successful demon hunter. But once you were born, she took you in and gave up her career to protect you."

I gaped at her, my heart speeding. "Wait, you knew Aunt Paula? You knew about me?" Professor Martha looked out the window. Many questions sprang to my mind. "Why wasn't I raised in this world? Why wasn't I trained as a demon hunter from the start? Why did my aunt hide this from me?"

"Even if I knew the answers to your questions, I'm in no position to answer them," she said. Her hard, hazel eyes turned back to me. "Since you're here, you might as well start classes tomorrow." Professor Martha sat in the chair behind the desk. She flipped through some papers, then filled out a form and scribbled something. "Here." She extended the paper to me. "This is your class schedule."

Slowly, I took a few steps forward and snatched the sheet of paper from her. "Martial arts, weapon's forging ... What the—?"

"I'll be your advisor, but you will be expected to arrive on time to all of your classes," she said, cutting me off once again. "I know this is all new to you, but your progress will be closely monitored, so try your best." I gulped, not sure what to say. She went on. "Because of your age, you'll be placed in the second-year class, which means, you'll have a lot to catch up on, and I trust you're mature enough to do it by yourself. However, since most elective classes are already full, you'll have one class with the third years, and one with the fourth." She pointed to the paper in my hands. "You'll find your dormitory building, the Gardenia building, and room number in the corner. I wrote down some directions to make it easier to find. I'll send someone to your room later with your uniform and books." She waved her hand at me. "You're dismissed."

I stared at her. That was it? She wasn't going to tell me more about this place, explain the rules, or anything else? She was pushing me out the door without wishing me luck?

What a great advisor.

Feeling lost and a little angered, I walked out of her office and walked back the way Rey and I had come in. I paused in the foyer. I glanced at the paper in my hand and read the directions to the dorm. Exit the Aster building through the back door, turn left on the stone path, follow the signs for the—

I rolled my eyes, an urge to crumple the paper and throw it away hitting me hard. What else could I do, though? Without much of a choice, I followed the directions Professor Martha had written down.

Once outside the Aster building, I halted and gawked at the giant tree taking over the center of the courtyard between several buildings. Its trunk and branches were black, and there were no leaves, just winding branches, vines, and thorns. Lots and lots of thorns.

Blackthorn.

Was this where the academy's name came from?

All right, enough with the questions. My mind would implode with them. All I needed to do was find my room, read through my schedule, and make sure I knew it by heart.

I resumed walking, following the directions.

I paused again at a tall, black signpost. There it was, the Gardenia building, to the right, just as Professor Martha's directions said. I turned that way and saw a student with long, silver-blond hair walking in the opposite direction. Her eyes met mine and a small grin overtook her lips. The way she walked and stared at me, she looked like a model on a catwalk. She was even pretty enough for that. I thought she would walk past me, but when she stopped right in front of me, I braced myself.

"You must be Emily," she said, her voice dripping with fake sugar.

"Erin," I corrected her.

"I'm Ava Heyward." She flipped her hair back. "You've been here for what, not even thirty minutes, and the academy is already filled with rumors of your arrival. I think this is the first time I've ever heard of someone your age finding out about our world." She leaned in closer. "Tell me, do you have delusions that you'll fit in here?"

I gaped at her. "Excuse me?"

"I'm betting you won't last a week." She winked at me, then resumed her strut, walking away.

Shocked, I stared for a moment. Then, I rushed through the directions, eager to get out of the open and avoid any other students.

I found my dorm on the second floor of a dull, gray building. I stepped inside and locked the door. I tried to focus on the room and its furniture and arrangement—the twin bed, the nightstand, the desk and chair, the small walk-in closet, the adjacent bathroom—but it was too much. My feelings simmered inside me, and I was blind to everything else, but them. There was so much going on inside me, I didn't think I could deal with them, not all at once.

But right at this moment, the predominant feeling was loneliness. I had lost my aunt, Rey had abandoned me, and Professor Martha and Ava weren't welcoming.

I sat on the bed, and despite fighting them with all my might, the tears came, stronger this time.

6

REY

I FELT AWFUL ABOUT DROPPING ERIN WITH PROFESSOR Martha, but the sooner I distanced myself from her, the better. My life was fucked up, and I didn't need to drag her down with me.

I had taken a shower and changed into the academy workout uniform—sweatpants and T-shirt—when someone showed up at my dorm to deliver a message.

"Headmaster Randall is calling you for a meeting," Peter said. He was a second-year student who was great at martial arts, but he lacked the discipline to dedicate himself to the other subjects. He barely passed the final exams last school year.

"Thanks, Peter."

I looked down at myself. I should probably change into the regular uniform, or even one of my suits, but right now, I was in the mood to get on Randall's nerves.

Although I was a fourth-year student, Randall had picked me two years ago to follow in his footsteps, to be his second in command. According to him, he might want to retire someday and someone would need to take over the academy.

At first, I was ecstatic with the prospect of being close to him, to learn everything I could to report to Asmodeus, but Randall wasn't a fool. He knew I was half-demon and often threatened to tell the others about it. At least, he didn't know who exactly my father was, or I doubt he would tolerate me.

To be honest, I didn't know why he tolerated me at all. He was the first demon hunter, the founder of the academy. He should have struck me down the moment he found out the truth about me.

I always wondered if he thought he could use me. Like if there were others out there like me, he could use me to bring them to his side. I could only guess.

As I walked toward the Aster building, where Randall's office was located, I analyzed the situation. If he was alone, this would be a great opportunity to kill him. The sooner I got that done, the sooner I could stop pretending to be a fucking demon hunter, and the sooner I could regain my freedom.

The sooner Asmodeus and his demons would invade the academy and kill all the students and hunters.

Kill Erin.

For some reason, I didn't like that.

When I got to his fancy office, Randall wasn't alone. Professor Martha was with him and she was discussing Erin.

"I already took care of it," Professor Martha said. She noticed my presence and glanced at me.

"Sorry for barging in," I said, halting by the door. "I thought Randall was alone."

"It's okay." Professor Martha beckoned me to come in. "Rey was the one who found her, actually."

Seated on his throne-like chair behind his desk, Randall narrowed his eyes. "A new demon hunter? I wonder how she made it out there by herself."

"She had an aunt," I explained as I closed the door and approached the desk. "She was killed by a Garrach moments before I found Erin." Garrach was the bigger leader of the Garrimps, the little imps who attacked Erin.

Professor Martha looked down.

Randall tsked. "Since you're her advisor, Professor Martha, I trust you'll find out everything about her, and take care of her needs here at the academy." His voice was as calm and leveled as always. Though his short hair was gray, there weren't any wrinkle lines around his dark eyes. With his impressive height and straight back, he didn't look a day over thirty.

"Yes, sir," Professor Martha said.

Randall turned to me. "Welcome back to the academy, Rey," he said. "Ready for your fourth and final year?"

I nodded. "Yes, sir."

"Good." Randall stood. "The others should be arriving soon." With elegant and long steps, the headmaster rounded his desk and took a seat at the end of the sleek black table taking up half of the office. "Come," he told us.

Professor Martha sat at Randall's left, and I took my usual place—at the other end of the table.

Not a minute later, Professor Crimson, Professor Eleanor, and Professor Graham arrived and took their usual places. So, this was a meeting.

"What's this about?" Professor Crimson asked. He was a middle-aged hunter with a stick up his ass. That was the only explanation I had for how boring and uptight he was.

Randall didn't seem frazzled. "I called you all here to

discuss security at the school. While our students were out this summer, more and more demons have attempted to break through our barriers and invade the academy. Now that our students are back and classes commence tomorrow, we need to reinforce the magic around the school and increase the guards patrolling the grounds."

Professor Crimson scoffed. "If demons are being this daring, it's because they believe they can break in."

Professor Martha narrowed her eyes. "Are you suggesting something?"

"I'm not suggesting," Professor Crimson said. "I'm saying it. Headmaster Randall's powers aren't what they used to be."

Here we go again, I thought to myself, while suppressing a groan. It was no secret that Professor Crimson desired the position of headmaster. He had for many years now. Because of that, he started arguments with Randall all the fucking time. I didn't know why Randall put up with him. If it had been me, I would have fired him a long time ago.

"Crimson, if you would like, I'll take you up on a duel right now," Randall said, knowing all too well the other man wouldn't accept. No one in their right mind would duel with Randall.

That was why my current mission was so fucked up.

Professor Crimson shook his head. "We can't duel in here."

"Then let's take this outside, to the courtyard."

"What about the Blackthorn tree?" Professor Crimson asked. He always came up with the worst excuses. If he really wanted to take up Randall's mantle, he should start by not being such a chicken.

"Can you two please stop?" Professor Martha interceded. She was usually the most serious of all of us, and the one that broke them apart before their petty arguments turned into a brawl. "You're acting like children again. Please, put your differences aside and think about what's best for the school."

"Right," Professor Eleanor said. "We were talking about school security."

Randall fixed the tie of his suit, as if he really had rolled up his sleeves and gotten ready for a fight, and sat back in his chair. "Right, where were—?"

His words died when shadows emerged from the corner of his office.

Darkelth, a neutral demon, known for being able to sneak into places undetected. However, here in the academy, we had special protection that should have detected their presence.

Randall, the professors, and I jumped off our chairs as the shadows shaped into tall and lean humanoids with pitch black skin, a skeletal face, and horns on their bald heads. Their eyes sockets were hollow, and their mouths were a long slit from side to side, filled with sharp fangs.

"What the—?" Randall shouted. "Kill them!"

The professors and I called our Dawnblades, the dark blade appearing the moment our arms extended at our sides. Without waiting for them to advance, I lunged at the nearest demon.

With six of us, strong as we were, the neutral demons had no chance. In a matter of seconds, we had cut through them and cleared the room.

Holding our breath, we waited a few more minutes, in case there were more hidden. But after a while, it was obvious there weren't any demons left.

"What was that?" Professor Martha asked. "Darkelth

inside the academy is unacceptable. Or any kind of demon, for that matter."

"Exactly my point," Randall said, sitting in his chair again. He held his sword with both hands. His sword wasn't like ours. It was jet black with a wavy blade, and the hilt looked like a broken branch. Despite its simple look, his sword was powerful. It had come directly from the Blackthorn tree, like the first generation of demon hunters' swords had. Now, we didn't get them from the tree, but we magically forged them. "There should never be demons in here."

I waited for him to cut me a look, but he didn't.

"What do we do now?" Professor Eleanor asked. "Should we do a campus-wide search to make sure no more Darkelth are hiding inside the academy?"

"That's a good idea," Professor Graham agreed.

"It is, but it's not enough." Randall lowered his sword. "I'm putting Rey in charge of security."

"What?" Professor Crimson shrieked. "I've tolerated his invites to our meetings, and his input, but Rey is a student. He shouldn't have any authority."

Randall leaned forward on the table, his elbows on the smooth black top. "I'm the headmaster and I trust Rey. He is on his way to becoming the greatest demon hunter this academy has ever seen, and I am putting him in charge of security." He turned his eyes to me. "Make sure those demons are gone and that none of them can enter this academy."

I nodded. "Yes, sir."

"Meeting dismissed," Randall said, waving his hand at us.

Because I didn't want to hear Professor Crimson bitching about me, I was the first out of the office. I was sure to lose my temper and do something I would regret later. So, I kept walking, until I was sure I was far away from them. Feeling like I was being pulled in several directions, I halted in front of the Blackthorn tree and stared at its black thorns.

How would I be able to secure the campus and kill Randall at the same time? If I did one, it meant I was giving up on the other.

Letting out a sigh, I went back inside the Aster building and headed toward the security office.

Killing Randall could wait for now.

7

ERIN

LAST NIGHT, AFTER CRYING MORE THAN I HAD EVER CRIED before, I decided I wouldn't freaking cry anymore. Every time I thought about my aunt, sorrow and guilt overwhelmed me, but I fought through it. Crying wouldn't change anything. All I could do now was honor her by trying my best and becoming as good as she was.

But that didn't mean I felt ready for this.

I glanced down at my class schedule. I must have read the thing three hundred times since yesterday afternoon.

Last evening, a woman brought me clothes, books, pens, other class materials I would need, toiletries, and some snacks. I was especially thankful for the food, because then I could skip going to the cafeteria for breakfast this morning. Although I was rather eager to meet the other students, I didn't think the cafeteria was the best place for it.

Every few seconds, Ava and the way she treated me crossed my mind. If all the students were like her, I was screwed.

All right, I shouldn't worry about that now. I was here,

wasn't I? I couldn't hide in my room. All I had to do was think this was like going to college. I had wanted to go to one so freaking bad; this was my chance.

Although, training to be a demon hunter was somewhat cooler than becoming a lawyer, a dentist, or a teacher.

For all the classes, female students were supposed to wear a white shirt, dark green tie, black jacket, and a black and green pleated skirt, with white socks and black shoes. But for my first class, martial arts, we were supposed to wear black tactical pants, a black thermal tee, and black combat boots— what was up with all the black?

Dread and nervousness filled me as I made my way to the Hyacinth building at the end of campus, where the class was held—this building housed the gym and combat training facilities too. It got worse when I saw the other students, walking to their classes.

How could I be so eager about something, but also so worried?

Trying to keep my nervousness under control, I entered the building and found the assigned classroom. It was a large room with mats on the floor and one wall covered in mirrors.

The students, all dressed like me, were already inside, most of them gathered in small groups, either stretching or chatting, or both.

I dragged my feet inside and found a spot near the wall, where I could pretend I was one more person. But I wasn't, and it was obvious they all had already heard about the new girl, because they kept firing glances at me and whispering.

Ava was there. She stood near the mirrors with two other girls. Staring at me, she said something to her friends, then they all laughed.

I puffed out my chest, determined not to crumble, and started stretching my arms, shoulders, and neck.

Not a minute later, a woman with a long, gray braid, and plump red lips walked in. She wore a black suit with a green shirt—the professors' uniform.

She walked with sure steps to the center of the room. The students promptly circled her, all ready for whatever she was going to say. I scooted closer, but didn't push my way through.

"All right, this is what we'll be working on today," said the professor, whose name I still didn't know. She beckoned a male student to come to her. The young man walked in a circle and stood in front of her, his feet apart, his hands up. "Attack me, Peter," she said.

Peter rushed at her, his fist ready to land a punch. The professor took a small step back, parried his incoming arm with her hand, closed her fingers around his wrist, twisted his arm out and away from her body, hit him with her elbow, and landed a kick to his chest. All her movements were controlled and precise, and I bet she wasn't really hitting him that hard —then she hooked that same leg on his ankle, bringing him down.

"Ouch," he muttered.

"If the supernatural you're fighting seems like he'll stand up after that, then you can land a punch." The professor crouched down and demonstrated, her fist stopping a centimeter from the student's face. "Or you can stomp on the sensitive areas." She stood and brought her foot to his crouch. Peter brought his hands down, protecting that area.

A few students chuckled, but the professor cut them a hard look. "Understood?" she asked, looking around.

"Yes, Professor Genevieve," everyone replied.

At least, I knew her name now.

"Then get to work." She clapped once and the class dispersed. "Erin Delman." Her voice was hard, as if she was ready to reprimand me.

"Yes?" I walked to her.

"I understand you're a new student, but to remain in my class, you'll have to catch up," she said.

"I'll do my best," I told her, being honest.

"Ava Heyward," the professor called.

The blonde bitch skipped to us. "Yes, Professor Genevieve?"

"Since you're one of my best students, pair up with Erin today," the professor said. My eyes widened. Hell no! "Please, teach her some basic moves, then move on to today's exercise."

"My pleasure," Ava said, a fake smile plastered on her face. The professor walked away, and Ava turned to me, her fake grin still on her face. "Are you ready to have your ass kicked?"

I groaned on the inside. "It won't matter if I ask you to go easy, right?"

"Right." She didn't give me time to think. She lunged at me. Unprepared, I stood there as she landed a punch to my gut, then swiped my feet from underneath me.

I crashed to the mat. Pain radiated through my back, and the air rushed out of my lungs.

What a freaking piece of shit.

Slowly, I got up. The moment I stood upright, Ava was on me again. This time, I was expecting it and stepped to the side. I tried the technique Professor Genevieve had showed us, but I wasn't fast enough. Even if I had been fast, I wasn't sure what I was doing, or trying to do.

Ava brought me down again.

She chuckled, watching as I groaned on the floor.

I glanced at the professor. She walked around the room, stopping here and there, correcting some stances and moves from other students. She had looked our way, but if she noticed Ava, she didn't care.

So that was how this was going to be?

I took my time standing up, but once more, the moment I had both my feet under me, Ava jumped me. I moved a little faster this time, but I only lasted a second longer than before.

She was an experienced fighter, or at least much more experienced than me. I had never been in a fight or had self-defense lessons before. At this point, I couldn't fight. I tried my best to stay up for as long as I could, but Ava always brought me down.

By the end of the class, I had hit the floor about a hundred times, if not more.

When the class was dismissed, all the students walked out as if nothing had happened. Well, this was a normal class for them, after all.

I couldn't move, though. Hurting all over, I stayed sprawled on the mat, trying to calm my breathing. Shit. If it hurt this bad now, I couldn't imagine how bad it would be later today. Or tomorrow.

I wanted to close my eyes and take a nap, but my next class started in less than ten minutes, and I still had to stop by my room and change clothes.

Pain shot up my legs with each step I took, but I had to rush.

I arrived in the classroom for my next class, demon history, with thirty seconds to spare. This classroom looked like an auditorium: desks and chairs that formed a semicircle around a long black table at the bottom of the room, and a white board behind it that filled most of the wall.

There was one open spot right in the middle of the room. I sat down, only two seconds before the professor walked into the room.

"Y-you're the new girl," someone said in a low voice.

I glanced at the girl sitting beside me. She had huge green eyes, black framed glasses, and soft, brown curls. There were lots of books and notebooks spread in front of her, more than I thought we would need for this class.

"Yes. I'm Erin."

"I'm Claire," she said with a smile. "Welcome to the Blackthorn Hunters Academy."

I tilted my head. Could this girl actually be nice? Or was she playing a trick on me?

"All right," the professor said loudly. The first thing I noticed about him was that he was short and stocky. He had messy black hair and thin glasses that rested on the tip of his long nose. "This year, we'll be reviewing the years 483 to 561 BC, when there were some interesting wars in the supernatural world. Please open your books to chapter one."

This class was much easier than my previous one. At least, this one I didn't need to get my butt kicked. Professor Graham—his name was written on the sheet he passed around the class—read some of chapter one and explained a little more about it. Then, he told us to gather in pairs or trios for the upcoming project, which was explained on the sheet he had handed to us.

"Want to be my partner?" Claire asked, her voice soft.

"Sure," I said, genuinely content about pairing up with her. She looked like she was good at studying, and so far, she had been nice to me.

"Cool." She wrote our names on another sheet and passed it along, so other students could sign it. When class was dismissed, she turned to me. "What do you have now?"

"Nothing," I said. "Not until later in the afternoon, I think."

"I'm heading to the cafeteria for an early lunch. Want to join me?"

"I would love to."

Walking out of the classroom with Claire, I felt so relieved. Despite my rough start, I had finally made a friend. I wasn't alone in this place anymore! While we walked to the cafeteria, I told her about Ava.

"Oh, yeah, she can be nasty," Claire said, nodding. "I'm sorry about her."

I shrugged. "It's okay. I'm sure she'll get bored with me soon and move on." At least, I hoped so.

"At the beginning of last year, our first year here, she used to pick on me," Claire confessed. "I'm awkward and quiet, and I don't make friends easily. I'm also terrible when it comes to physical activities, and Ava picked up on that. Being a super-lithe athletic girl, she chose me for sparring once. Let's just say I wanted to run away from class and cry." She took a deep breath. "So, yeah, I know exactly what you're feeling."

"That blonde bitch," I said through gritted teeth.

Claire chuckled. "I like that. Blonde bitch. It's like the perfect nickname."

Then, her smile faded and her face paled. I followed her line of sight and saw a professor walking straight to us. He was tall, with short brown curls and dark green eyes, which reminded me of—

"Claire," he said, a snap to his voice. "Did you turn in your report?"

"Not yet, I still have ti—"

"The report is due in two days."

"I know," she said. "It's done. I just need to—"

"Don't make me repeat myself," he said, cutting her off again. "I expect to see it on my desk by the end of the afternoon. Understood?"

Claire lowered her head. "Yes, professor."

The professor turned his cold gaze to me. He huffed at me, as if I was a bug that was contaminating the school, then walked away.

The moment he was gone, Claire let out a long breath.

"Who was that jerk?" I asked, still in shock about the way he treated her.

"That's Professor Crimson," she said, bringing her eyes to mine. "My father."

My jaw fell to the ground. "What? Oh, shit ... sorry. I shouldn't have called him a jerk." Where was a hole in the ground when you needed one?

"It's okay. It's true," she muttered. "He never hides his disappointment in me. He wishes I was strong and outgoing and popular like Ava." She gestured to herself. "But this is all he got."

I waved her off. "I would rather have ten of you than one of Ava."

She smiled, but it didn't reach her eyes. "Thanks."

I hooked my arm with hers and tugged her forward. "Weren't we going to the cafeteria? I'm hungry."

She nodded and started walking with me. "Right. Let's go."

Claire led the way. The cafeteria was on the bottom floor

of the female dorm. Most of the walls were made of glass, and as we walked closer, I could see it was already full of students. And here I was hoping that, if we got there a little early, we would be the only ones there.

"Ugh, is it always this crowded?" I asked, slowing my steps.

"Pretty much," Claire said. "Don't worry. Just do what I do. Ignore them all. That way, they will ignore you too."

If only that was true.

I let out a long breath and went in with her, ready to brave another jungle.

8

I spent the night going around campus, making sure the magic was holding up, the thorns around the walls were sharp, the cameras were working, and the guards were patrolling the right areas. Fortunately, there weren't any more Darkelth inside the school, but I still didn't understand how they got in.

And inside Randall's office nonetheless, which was the heart of the academy. If it had been near the outer walls ... it still didn't make sense.

Because of my demon blood, I didn't need much sleep, but I was still fucking tired from being awake for so long and working all night, when I went to my first class of the semester.

Weapon forging. It was an elective class that most third years took. I had skipped it last year, because of my duties as Randall's second, but it was a class I was really looking forward to, so I signed up for it, even though I was already in the fourth year.

The class was held in a large classroom with several desks

in the middle and stone forges in the back. One of the walls was large glass doors, which opened when we worked the forges.

Since I didn't have any other classes before this one, I arrived early. Slowly, students started pouring in. Like I predicted, most were third years. Except for the girl with black hair and pretty golden eyes.

Erin entered the classroom, throwing me off. I hadn't expected to see her in this class. Because of her age, she was a second-year student, but she should have been assigned to first-year electives. What was Professor Martha thinking?

Her eyes met mine. She paused for a moment, then took a sharp turn and sat in an empty spot in the back.

A few minutes later, Professor Astrid walked in. She was a short woman of about sixty, who seemed too fragile to hold a fork in her hand, much less handle the heavy weapons we made. But despite her appearance, I knew she was agile and clever for her age.

"All right, students," she called. "Because of the number of forges we have, I'll need you to pair up. Pay attention to the names I call. You'll be working together for the rest of the year." She started rattling off names until only two were left. "Erin Delman and Rey Lowe, because you two are the only ones who aren't in the third year, you'll use forge number twelve."

What the fuck?

An urge to glance at Erin hit me, but I held strong. But once the professor told us to move to the forges, I had no choice. All I wanted was to avoid her for the rest of the semester, and yet, here I was, walking to her desk.

"Hey," I said, feeling incredibly lame.

"Hi." Erin closed her notebook. "Should I just leave my things here?"

"Yeah, you won't need any of that at the forge."

We walked to forge twelve, the closest one to the open glass doors. From here, we could see the extensive courtyard and a hint of the Blackthorn tree in the distance.

Erin stared at the forge as if it were a monster. I swallowed a chuckle before it slipped past my lips.

"If a year ago someone had told me I would one day forge a weapon, I would have thought that person was on crack," she muttered.

I could only imagine how she felt right now.

For some reason, I felt like helping her out. "First, we should turn it on," I said, reaching for the little metal door underneath the stone forge. I showed her the button and knob beside the door. "This is where we turn the fire on." I clicked the button and fire sparked to life. "And we control the temperature with this." I turned the knob until it was set to four hundred degrees. That was enough for now.

"Tell me there's a magical option," she said, staring at the fire. "Like, a menu where I choose which weapon I want. Then, I throw some metal inside the forge, and the chosen weapon is spat out a few minutes later, all ready and pretty."

This time, I chuckled. "That is a neat idea, but no, there's no easy path." I turned to the big crate in front of the forge, with lots of metal pieces inside. "First, we need to decide what you want to make." I looked at her. "You don't have a Dawnblade yet, do you?" I tsked. "But we would need more time to do one of those." I picked up the metal that had already been cut. "This could work as a nice dagger."

"I'm lost here," she said. "I'm okay with whatever you choose."

She was overwhelmed; I got it. I would let her off the hook and just show her everything today, but I would certainly require her to be more hands-on in the next class.

"All right, let's do a dagger, then." I cut the end of the metal for the tang, about eight inches long. "This is called a leaf," I said, showing her the piece I had chosen. "This is different from what it'll be in the end."

To mold the leaf into the blade I wanted, I put it in the fire, then used a hammer to shape it. All the while, Erin stood right by my side, just over my shoulder, watching everything with attention. I was aware of her so close by, of her rose scent tickling my nose, of how sexy she looked in that ridiculous collegial uniform.

Next, I worked on annealing the blade, then grinding. Because the class was only two hours long, we didn't have time to finish the dagger, but I felt like we had made good progress.

"I confess, it seems like hard work, but it's also pretty cool," Erin said, as we walked out of the classroom. "Is that how you make a Dawnblade?"

"Yes, and no," I said. "A Dawnblade uses a magical metal, so we don't need a lot of melting and shaping, but it's still hard work and a long process."

She frowned. "Do all students have a Dawnblade?"

"They receive it when they start classes the first year. You should talk to Professor Martha. I'm sure she can have one made for you."

Brows still curled down, she nodded. Then, she picked up a sheet of paper and read it. She halted and glanced around. "I have to meet Claire at the library to start working on our project." She looked down at the paper again. I leaned a bit closer and saw it was a campus map. "It's that way, right?"

"Not quite." I placed my finger on the map. "We're here." I dragged my fingertip to another point on the map. "And here is the library, in the Iris building."

"Oh." She sighed. "This place is so huge. I'm still lost." She started walking away. "Thanks."

"Wait," I called before I could stop myself. "Come on. I'll show you another way to get there."

Erin hesitated, but she ended up following me. I took her down a narrow stone path that cut between the dorms and rounded near the outer northwest wall. It was isolated here, and it made the walk twice as long, but there was something here I thought she would like to see.

Before this class, the last time I had seen her was when I dropped her at Professor Martha's office. It had been only yesterday, but for some reason, it felt longer than that. At the time, I wanted to get away from her, for her own safety.

I should still keep my distance. I should keep our interactions to the classroom, but I didn't want to. She wasn't saying or doing much, but I was enjoying her company.

Wanting to hear her voice, I asked, "Should I ask you how your first day was?"

She groaned. "Not good. Well, it depends actually." She told me about sparring with Ava and having her ass kicked. Then about meeting Claire and finally making a friend. She also told me about bumping into Professor Crimson and being shocked at how he treated his daughter.

"He's like that with everyone, but worse with Claire," I told her.

Next, she told me about lunch in the cafeteria and how everyone stared at her. For some reason, I felt like stopping there tomorrow during lunchtime and sitting with her. I was sure they wouldn't stare then.

But that was something I shouldn't do. I shouldn't even be showing her this shortcut. I should have sent her to the library and gone to my next class.

"Then, you know, the weapon forging class," she said. "I confess it sounds super cool, but I'm still intimidated by it all. Just looking at that forge makes me nervous."

I fought off a grin. "I could tell."

She shook her head. "Sorry. You asked me about my day, but I'm sure you didn't expect a full report. It's just ... I'm so overwhelmed. Sorry."

"It's okay. I understand." To my dismay, I wanted to know the details of her day.

Suddenly, the neat green grass changed into bushes of black vines, thorns, and red roses. The red roses had magically been inserted among the bushes, just to make them prettier, and right now, they reminded me of Erin—of her beauty and her sweet scent.

"This place is incredible," she said, spinning around, her amused gaze on the rosebushes.

I fought a smile. "Glad you like it."

She halted and looked at me, her eyes narrowed. "Are you showing me this on purpose?"

I brought my hand to my neck, not sure how to answer that. But before I could, something prickled my skin. I sensed it a split-second before it appeared. A muttmaug jumped out from behind a bush along the outer wall. Erin screamed. With an arm out to protect her, I twisted out of the way. The gray-green-skinned creature kept coming, snarling. Standing on all fours, the muttmaug looked like a big, furless wolf, and instead of ears, it had two big, curling horns.

My Dawnblade appeared in my hand.

As if by magic, two more muttmaug appeared beside the first one.

"What the fuck?" I muttered, confused. I had reviewed the security for the entire campus. There couldn't be any demons inside the academy. "Erin, stay back."

The first demon lunged at me. I spun out of the way, my blade wide, and slashed across its chest. It fell to the ground, black blood staining the stone path. The second one shrieked before attacking me. I ducked under its claw, turned around, and pierced my sword into his back. I didn't wait for the third demon to attack. Sword raised high, I rushed to it.

But this one was smart. Instead of coming for me, it went for Erin.

At first, Erin stared at it, frozen. But a second later, she acted. She threw the thickest of her books right at its head, then ran toward me. I smiled as the demon shook his head, apparently dizzy from the hit, then turned to me. But I was already a foot from him and cutting through his midriff.

I stepped back, taking in three corpses on the ground. Three demons. These three demons had been able to break through my tight security, and they attacked me. Didn't they know who I was? As a half-demon, they should be able to sense me. They wouldn't attack me for no reason.

Unless there was some other big name in the underworld trying to undermine Asmodeus's plans.

That was the only explanation I could come up with right now.

I turned around and found Erin with her hands over her face. She spied through the cracks of her fingers.

"They are gone," I told her.

"I know, but the bodies and the blood ... it's just too gory."

I picked up her book. It was dripping with black blood. "I think we'll need to get you a new book."

She lowered her hands a little, keeping them over her nose and mouth. "Oh, shit, that's nasty."

I dropped the book beside the corpses. I needed to investigate what was going on, and then send someone to clean this mess up. But first ... first I needed to send Erin away. If there were demons lurking, then it was too dangerous for her.

"Erin, I need you to go," I said. She dropped her arms. I pointed behind her. "Just follow this path and you'll be back at the main courtyard in less than a minute. Actually, you should run."

"But, what about you?"

"I need to investigate this," I told her.

She frowned. "Investigate?"

"Long story short, I'm more than a student at the academy, and right now, I'm in charge of campus security." I pointed to the mess beside us. "This is my responsibility."

"I see," she said, her voice low. Disappointed. She was disappointed. About what?

"I just ... I can't worry about your safety right now," I tried to explain. "I would feel better if you're with the other students and professors, instead of here, where another demon could appear."

Erin took a step back. "I get it."

"One more thing," I said, feeling like a jerk. "Please don't tell anyone. I don't want people freaking out."

"Okay." Her eyes fell to the mess behind me again, and her nose wrinkled. "Just ... be careful."

She spun on her heels and dashed away.

I watched her for a moment, wishing I could say more. I did want her gone, but I also wanted her near me. Which was wrong, so very wrong. After I saw her at the end of the path, where it joined the main path again, I turned my attention to the corpses at my feet.

Were these the only demons on campus? And just how did they get inside? I marched to the nearest guard outpost, where the campus guards stood, watching over the wall, and from where they patrolled the estate. There were several outposts—tall stone towers—spread out along the estate's perimeter, and the nearest one was only a few yards from where I stood, hidden by thick bushes and tall trees.

Fuck.

There was red blood smeared at the outpost entrance, and the scent of death was thick. I braced myself and walked in. As I expected, the guards had been slaughtered. The cameras here were turned off, and the magic was weak.

Double, triple fuck. Randall would have my neck for this. And since I had just increased security and made sure this wasn't supposed to happen, I would have to accept the consequences.

But after that, I would make sure no demon entered this damn academy anymore.

At least, not until I fulfilled Asmodeus's wishes by killing Randall and invited them all in.

9

ERIN

I COULDN'T SAY THINGS GOT BETTER AS THE WEEKS PASSED, BUT I think I learned how to deal with most of it.

In martial arts class, I wasn't paired with Ava anymore. But I was so far behind that it didn't matter who my sparring partner was; I still got my butt kicked.

Demon history always gave me a headache. Since I had missed the previous year of school, I had to study for both this year and last year—Claire helped me with that late at night at the library—so I understood what was going on in my textbook.

Speaking of books—when Rey showed me the shortcut to the library two weeks ago and we were attacked by that demon, I had thrown my demon history book at it. That same night, a new book arrived at my dorm. No notes, no explanation, but I could only gather that Rey had sent it to me.

And that always reminded me of the way he told me to go that day. I understood why he had done it. He was the head of security at the academy and he had much more experienced fighting than I did. If more demons showed up, then he would be distracted trying to save me. Still, I couldn't help feeling disappointed that he had asked me to leave.

As he requested, I had kept quiet about the attack. During one of our weapon forging classes, Rey told me he had dealt with that issue and tightened security. And that was practically all he said to me in the last two weeks, other than class matters, like the forge temperature and which kind of hammer to pick to mold the metal this way or that way.

Since the beginning, he had been hot or cold. One moment, he was taking care of me. The next, he was abandoning me entirely. I should have been used to it by now. I should just go with the flow and not care. But I did care. Maybe it was because he had saved me that night and brought me here, but I felt like we had shared something special.

Apparently, it was all in my head.

One unexpected thing that happened and I was immensely thankful for was having most of my things brought to me. As my advisor, Professor Martha said she would take care of my aunt's affairs. She had my things packed and delivered to my bedroom at the academy, along with a few other things: a few pictures of my aunt and me, her badass hunter clothes, which I guess she kept hidden, and her Dawnblade.

At first, my suite—our rooms were a nice-sized square with a small walk-in-closet and bathroom—felt crowded, but after I organized everything and even got rid of old clothes and shoes, it felt more like home. I placed my favorite picture of my aunt and me on the nightstand beside my bed. It was a simple picture of the two of us eating ice cream in the backyard of our house on my sixteenth birthday, but what made it so precious was that it had been a rare moment when the two of us had bright smiles on our lips. Looking back, I guess I had been happier growing up with her than I first thought.

Another thing I was grateful for was Claire. Since we first met, she had been by my side, and she was proving to be a great friend. She told me more about her family. Her mother died when she was a small child during a hunt, and her father was never the same. Growing up with him had been hard on her, and I guessed that was the reason why she was so quiet and shy. In return, I told her about me—the stupid dare that had brought me face-to-face with dangerous demons, my aunt who had been a demon hunter all her life and died trying to save me, and Rey who found me and brought me to the academy.

One morning, Professor Martha barged into my bedroom.

I glanced at my phone on the nightstand—the same one I wasn't allowed to use at the school. It was freaking four fifty-five in the morning. "What happened?" I sat up, startled. For her to be here, something bad must have happened.

"Get up," she said, her voice harsh even this early in the day. "Get dressed."

"What's going on?"

"We're training," she said. "Now."

Without another look at me, she walked out of the room. I stared at the door for a moment longer, a little lost. What the freaking what? Despite feeling the urge to argue and go back to sleep, I knew Professor Martha well enough to know she wouldn't let me off the hook. If she said we were training, then we were training, even if she had to drag me by my hair.

Grunting, I rolled out of bed and put on my tactical pants, thermal tee, and boots. I tied my hair into a tight ponytail, washed my face, brushed my teeth, and met her in the hallway.

"What about breakfast?" I asked her as we left the building. A chilly breeze rolled by and I hunched my shoulders. It was only September and it was already too cold in the mornings.

"When the training session is done," she said.

Holy shit, I was sure to hate whatever she had planned.

Professor Martha took me to the same classroom I had my martial arts class in. She stood in the middle of the mat, and only then did I realize she wasn't wearing her usual school suit, but clothes like mine. She set her feet apart and lifted her hands, closing them into fists.

"Whoa, so, you're just going to come at me?" I asked, so not up for this at this unholy hour of the day. If it wasn't for her stoicism, I would have given her the finger and stayed in bed.

"Since I've been hearing how one of my students is terrible at fighting, I will be teaching you proper fighting stances and basic technique. We'll build from there."

I frowned. "Why?"

"Why what?"

"Why do you care whether I fail?"

"Because I'm your advisor, and how you do reflects on me," she said, her tone curt. "Now, mirror my stance. Legs apart, hip width, knees slightly bent, core braced, arms and hands tights."

I did as she asked. "I already know how to position myself for a fight. The problem is the actual fight."

"First things first." She twisted to the side, landed a powerful side kick to my stomach. The air rushed from my lungs. I stumbled back, almost falling on my butt.

"Holy shit." I gasped for air and willed away the damn pain radiating through my stomach and chest.

"Depending on your opponent, his strength will be enough to destabilize you, but even then, you should be able to hold your own. If your legs are locked, if your abs are braced, you can take the hit without falling." She returned to the initial position. "Again."

I stared at her. "W-what? You're going to hit me again?"

"I am going to hit you until you wobble, but don't move your feet."

"That is torture," I snapped. Usually, I viewed myself as calm and easy-going. Until someone woke me up at five in the morning and wanted to beat me up.

"No, it's a lesson," she snapped. "You're the only student in the second-year martial arts class who can't hold her own. Even the ones who struggle, don't lose the fight five seconds after it's started. But you do. If you want to be a demon hunter, if you want to fight demons and not die, you need to pass that class with flying colors." She narrowed her eyes. "I've seen your grades, and if you keep going like this, you'll fail."

"You've seen my grades?" I asked, confused. I didn't even know we were already being graded.

"I'm your advisor; I know everything about you." I narrowed my eyes at her. Yes, from what I could gather from our first conversation, she did know a lot about me and my aunt, Paula, but she refused to tell me anything. She went on, "Do you want this? Do you want to be here and become a demon hunter?"

I thought for a moment. This place was part magical and exciting, but also confusing and terrifying. On one hand, there were the hard classes, the getting my ass kicked all the time, the bitches who liked to bother me, and the overall army-like discipline of this place. On the other, I had made a good friend, I slept in a nice bed, I ate good food, I learned cool stuff like magic theory and demon history, and I was part of a special society. I didn't feel like I belonged yet, but maybe that was what I was missing. If I trained harder, if I studied more, maybe the other students wouldn't look down on me so much, and I would feel like I was a part of it all.

The thought both excited me and made me anxious.

I inhaled deeply. "Yes, I want to become a demon hunter."

One corner of Professor Martha's lips curled up. "Then get ready. Let's try this again."

I spread my legs, locked them, braced my core, and waited for her attack. The first five times, I fell on my butt, but after a while, when I ignored the pain and the soreness, I started stumbling less.

Maybe soon, I would be able to take the hit and keep moving.

After two and a half hours of hard work, Professor Martha called it quits. "You have class at eight-thirty. You better go shower and have breakfast."

"Yes, ma'am," I said, breathing hard.

"Tonight, go to the weight lifting room," she told me. "I'll have a program ready for you."

"Weight lifting?" She wanted me to train *more*?

"Yes, you need to build strength to keep up with the other students," she said. "Go to sleep early, though. I'll meet you here again at five tomorrow morning."

With that, she marched out of the classroom.

Tired and disheartened, I laid down on the mat and tried to catch my breath.

* * *

"HANG ON, JUST ABOUT THIRTY MINUTES MORE," CLAIRE urged.

I laid my head on the book and closed my eyes. "I'm done. Too tired. Everything hurts. Can't move."

She chuckled.

Someone shushed us.

After our classes were done for the day, Claire and I met in the library so she could help me with the lessons I missed from the first year. When she first offered to tutor me, I had declined. I mean, I wouldn't put her through this just because I needed to study more. But when she proved to me she loved studying and reviewing the material, I accepted her offer.

"Didn't Professor Martha say you should work out before bed?" Claire whispered.

I groaned. Could I pretend I hadn't heard that? Today had been the first day of this new, crazy training schedule, and after being in classrooms all day, and studying more with Claire, I was brain and muscle dead. Even if I made it to the weight training room later, I doubted I could lift a freaking half-pound plate.

Holy shit, I couldn't imagine doing all of this again tomorrow.

"I don't wanna," I said with a grunt.

"I'm amazed that Professor Martha is doing this, though."

I turned my head, so my cheek was pressed to my book, and looked at Claire. "What do you mean?"

"Haven't you noticed how tough and cold she is?"

I nodded. "Yup."

"So, for someone who is so tough and cold, why would she bother waking a student up so early to train with her? It doesn't make sense."

"She told me that since she's my advisor; she's responsible

for me," I told her. "If I fail, it'll look bad on her, and she wants to impress the headmaster."

Claire's brows curled down as she seemed to consider this. "That makes sense, I guess." She nudged my shoulder with her elbow. "Come on. One more chapter and questions, and we can get out of here."

"I seriously think I'm done for today." Everything hurt. My legs, my arms, my core, and my butt from falling on it so many times. And my brain from trying to keep up with so many names and titles and codes and years. Demon history was no joke, and that was only one of the subjects I had to catch up on.

"No, no giving up," she said. "If you do this, I'll go with you while you work out."

"Shit, no, no working out for me tonight."

Claire pouted. "How about if I sneak into the kitchen and steal a bar of chocolate?"

I sat up. "Wait, can you do that?"

She put her finger over her lips. "Shh. I've done it once, last year. I had a bad argument with my father and needed something sweet. I was caught, but because of whose daughter I am, nothing was done. I bet they wouldn't do anything again." She smiled at me. "What do you think?"

Chocolate as a reward for another thirty minutes of studying and working out, or ditch it all and go to bed.

I so wanted some freaking chocolate, but I didn't think I had the strength to hold my pen upright.

I closed my book. "I think I'll pass."

Rey walked into the library. Wearing a black suit like the teachers, he was probably here as the head of security, not a student. Holy shit, with that tall frame and lean body, he looked so handsome, so strong, so serious.

He stopped by the front desk-slash-counter and talked to the lady who worked there. Everyone who worked at the academy was from demon hunter families, but didn't want to actively hunt demons, or they had failed their classes and were expelled from the academy. But because the human world was so different from the supernatural, they had decided to stay and work here instead of trying their luck somewhere else.

That was what would happen to me if I failed my classes. That, or I would tuck my tail between my legs and leave this place, pretending it never existed.

The woman grinned at Rey, but he didn't grin back. She opened a small door for him, and he stepped behind the counter. He leaned over a computer and worked on it, while the woman stayed right behind him.

"You know, every time he's around, you stare at him."

I turned wide eyes to Claire. "What? I do not!"

She chuckled. "Shh, don't raise your voice. And yes, you do."

"No, but ..." I glanced at the front desk again. Rey was still at the computer. "I just ..."

I didn't know what to say. Why did I keep staring at him? I mean, he was clearly handsome. Who wouldn't stare at him?

"See," Claire said. "You like him."

"No," I said automatically. I cleared my throat. "It's not like that. I just think he's handsome, that is all."

"I'll pretend I believe you," she said. Then, the amusement left her face, replaced by worry. "Are you sure you don't want to study more? If you're really hurting, we can stop by the infirmary at the Daffodil building and ask for something for pain."

"Nah, I'll be fine." I gathered my books in a pile, but my

action was lost when Rey stepped away from the computer. He said something to the woman, then walked out of the library. He didn't even see me. What did it matter if he saw me or not? It wasn't like we were friends. He had barely said a word to me even during class. I let out a long sigh. "Are you ready?"

"Give me two minutes." Claire leaned over her notebook and resumed writing.

I finished packing and waited for her, while staring at the front doors, as if Rey would be back here at any second. I was so freaking stupid for hoping something like that.

Rey didn't come into the library again, but Professor Genevieve rushed in. "Everyone! Please, may I have your attention," she said. All the students in the room turned to her. "All students are required to go to their rooms immediately."

Whispers spread through the library like wildfire.

"What happened?" a student named Peter asked.

The professor hesitated. "There has been an accident."

WHEN I WAS CALLED TO INVESTIGATE THE ACCIDENT, MY MIND went instantly to Erin. Was she okay? It hadn't been anything with her, right? I had just left the library and seen her there with Claire. She had been fine, tired, but fine.

As I followed Remi, the guard who called me, toward the place of the accident, I kept thinking it had to be demons. For the past couple of weeks, there hadn't been any other sightings or attacks on the school. My security detail seemed to be working.

And now this fucking accident.

But, as the guard took me to a corner of the Aster building, where a tall turret was located, I started doubting it had been demons.

"What happened?" I asked, approaching the white sheet spread over the stone pavement.

"A student," Remi said. "Brianne Charles. She fell from the top balcony."

"Fell?" I repeated. "Was she pushed? Or maybe suicide?"

"We don't know," Remi said.

I stepped closer to the white sheet. I knelt on the ground and pulled the sheet up. Her body was mangled from the fall, blood forming a pool around her, but there didn't seem to be any telltale signs—no bruising that could have been from another student, or punctures or bites or sharp slashes done by demons.

She could have been magically controlled, but other than Randall and me, there was no one else here who could wield magic—and only Randall knew of my abilities.

I dropped the sheet and stepped back.

"Take her body to the infirmary," I told the guards. "I'll have a physician do a full exam on her later." I turned to Remi. "Tape the area and block access to the balcony. I'm going to search the area."

"Yes, sir," he said.

I didn't take ten steps away from the scene before Randall burst through the front doors and marched toward me.

"What the hell happened here?" he shouted.

I tried to maintain my composure. "A girl fell from the turret balcony. There are no signs of struggle, and it doesn't seem to be the work of demons."

"Even if it isn't demons, this still affects the security of this academy, which you're responsible for." He clenched his fists. "Don't make me regret giving you this position, Rey. I can easily replace you."

Well, I wouldn't really mind that, but since I needed his trust, I needed to be close to him, I couldn't let him know that. "I'll find out what happened."

He jutted his finger in my face. "You better! This can*not* happen again."

Randall stalked away and I let out a long breath. Determined to get to the bottom of this, I searched the area for clues, but I couldn't find anything. Nothing on the inside of the turret, the stairs, the balcony, the rooms nearby, the outside, the ground ... all dead ends.

It was almost midnight when I stopped by the infirmary at the Daffodil building. Cecile, the female physician who was a retired demon hunter, told me she found nothing unusual with the girl's body. She had died from the fall, and like I suspected, there had been no signs of struggle.

So far, the only thing I could conclude was that it had been a suicide.

After making another round around the campus, checking all the gates and outposts, and making sure no students were out, I headed to my bedroom.

My body was exhausted from my classes, from the events of the evening, and from the frustration of having something so horrible happening at the academy without any real answer. But my mind wouldn't stop.

Since the students were in lockdown in their rooms, I would have to wait until tomorrow to interview the girl's friends. Maybe they could tell me if she was depressed, or if there could be any other situation in her life that would make her think suicide was an option.

I could be half-demon and try to act as if I didn't care, but it only hurt more and more when I did.

Once more, I had been thrust into a fucking impossible situation.

I had first entered this academy to obtain crucial information about the demon hunters. Then, Asmodeus ordered me to stay here. At the end of the third year, he had promised I wouldn't need to come back.

Yet, here I was, back at the academy with the insane mission of killing the headmaster. How would I kill a demon hunter, *the first* demon hunter, who had been alive for thousands and thousands of years and had unimaginable power?

The only way was getting even closer to him so I could learn his weaknesses. And that came with doing what he asked of me: protecting the academy against demons. As if he didn't know I was one.

Asmodeus's mission and Randall's assignment were opposing forces. Because of the end goal, I chose to follow Randall's orders first. Only then, I would be able to fulfill Asmodeus's wishes.

These thoughts create a fucking knot in my brain.

In my suite, I took a long, relaxing shower, and headed to bed. Because I was technically still a student, I stayed in the male dorms, the Snapdragon building. My bedroom was like any other in the building—a twin bed against the wall, a nightstand, a desk with a chair, a dresser, a bookcase, and a small loveseat—all in dark wood and green accents in the school colors. Plus, a walk-in closet and a private bathroom.

I closed my eyes and forced myself to sleep. My brain didn't quiet, though. Tired but too wired to sleep, I pulled out my book for the demonic spells class and read the assigned chapter for tomorrow's class.

The chapter talked about demonic pacts and that they could only be broken in three ways—by making another deal with the demon who made the pact, with the demon setting the victim free, or by the victim having a Soul Bond with someone who was their twin soul.

A twin soul meant two people whose spirits were identical. The chapter mentioned how Soul Bonds were somewhat like Immortal Vows, except that the Soul Bond happened by a chance of luck, while with the Immortal Vow, the duo chose each other as soulmates before their births.

The Soul Bond was more powerful than demonic magic and could break some curses. Although, twin souls were rare and practically unheard of.

Because of that, most demonic pacts ended with the victims' death.

I shut the book and threw it across the room.

What a fucking terrible chapter. It only added salt to my wound, reminding me that I had no way of escaping the contract with my father. Making another deal with Asmodeus was out of the question. He would only trick me in the end and add years to my forever-long contract. Meeting a twin soul was next to impossible. I had no hopes of finding a woman whose soul was identical to mine. Which left the only other option: The demon in question had to set me free. My only chance was to follow Asmodeus's orders and kill Randall, hoping my father would honor our deal.

I was so fucking screwed.

11

ERIN

LAST MORNING, I WAS PAIRED UP WITH AVA AGAIN IN MARTIAL arts, and she didn't waste time kicking my ass. Two days ago, I failed a quiz on magic spells. Three days ago, I dozed off in the middle of demon history and received a negative mark. Four days ago, I messed up in weapons forging class. I destroyed my entire blade and almost burned Rey in the process. Rey, who barely spoke to me, even in class. When I asked him about the accident and Brianne's death, he dismissed my questions.

A week ago, when we were ushered to our bedrooms and placed on lockdown all night, a girl had died on campus. From what we had heard, it had been suicide, but I had learned the headmaster had grilled Rey because of that. After all, he was the head of security at the academy.

Was that why he seemed to be in a worse mood? He was being punished somehow?

I hated seeing him like this and I kept wondering if I had done something wrong. He had seemed so open and friendly at first, and then suddenly, he was closed off and pushing me away.

Because of the accident, there was now a curfew. Students were supposed to be inside the dorms at eight in the evening, without excuses. That left everyone on edge.

On top of all that, Professor Martha still woke me up at five in the morning, even on weekends, and ran me through a training from hell. At night, she made sure I went back to the Hyacinth building, so I would do weight lifting—I had a special pass from her so I could skip curfew.

I was a walking zombie, dragging my feet everywhere and groaning in pain with each step.

I had been so excited about joining the academy, being part of something, making friends, and learning cool skills, but now, I wasn't so sure. Despite the good accommodations and great food, the classes were hard, the teachers were mean, and the students even meaner. Not to mention the demons. They were dangerous and powerful, much more than I could imagine. I couldn't see myself fighting one and winning. With the level of skills I knew now, I was sure I would lose, even to the little imps who attacked me back at that haunted house.

It hurt, because from the little Professor Martha had told me, my aunt had been an amazing demon hunter. I wanted to make her proud, but so far, I had only embarrassed myself. Embarrassed her.

"You don't look well," Claire said, as we walked toward our next class: potion making. It was my least favorite class. I had never been good with cooking, and mixing the ingredients to make potions was no different.

At least, we never made anything too complex. Because we weren't witches or warlocks—the latter a kind of supernatural who had recently resurfaced, or so I heard—and didn't have any magic, we couldn't make a large variety of potions, thank goodness.

I scoffed. "Try working out until almost eleven at night. Then, I couldn't sleep because of all the pain in my legs and core and arms. Oh, and let's not forget I was up and getting my ass kicked again at five in the morning."

She chuckled. I shot her a glare. "Sorry, it's just ... you're walking like a pregnant duck."

"Everything hurts!" I groaned.

"I know. I'm sorry." She patted my arm as we entered the classroom. We took our usual seats at a long table, and I instantly laid my head on my books. "Let's stop by my room after lunch," Claire said. "I have a tea that is supposed to be reenergizing. It might help."

I didn't believe much in teas, which was odd, since I was currently waiting for my potion class to start. If these freaking concoctions we put together were supposed to work, why wouldn't a simple herbal tea?

"Sure," I muttered, trying not to surrender to the sleep wanting to take me.

"Oh, no," Claire muttered.

"What?" I straightened in my chair and glanced up ahead. Professor Crimson, Claire's father, had marched in the room and halted behind the instructor's table. "What is he doing here?"

She shrugged. "I don't know."

"Attention," Professor Crimson said, his voice loud and hard, as usual. "Professor Wesley had an important appointment this morning and couldn't come to class, thus I'll be his substitute."

"Shit," I muttered.

"Open your books to chapter six," he said. "We'll be working on a truth elixir today."

Had I mentioned we never made complex potions in class? Well, this one was a complicated one.

Harvey, the student who broke the most hearts at the academy, raised his hand. "Professor Crimson, Professor Wesley said we wouldn't be making those kinds of potions in class."

"Well, Professor Wesley isn't here, is he?" Professor Crimson barked. "Now, get to work!"

A rubber band had been pulled tight across the classroom as every student opened their books and started to read the potion's instructions. It seemed I wasn't the only one who didn't like Professor Crimson. Or rather, was afraid of him. I had heard rumors he was close to the headmaster, which meant if he badmouthed a student, it could be that student's end.

Why, oh shit, why, had Professor Crimson subbed for my least favorite class?

Tension spread through my body as I made my way back to the shelves with the other students and gathered the ingredients necessary for this potion—aster, benzoin, hemlock, mandrake, and few others.

Holding my breath, I started working on my potion. First, I added mugwort and hemlock to the mortar and used a pestle to crush them.

My nervousness only increased when Professor Crimson decided to walk around the class, pausing every three steps, narrowing his eyes at whatever we were doing, but not saying anything.

Holy shit.

The minutes dragged, but at the same time, I prayed I

finished in time. I sure didn't want to be the last to finish, otherwise Professor Crimson wouldn't miss the opportunity to chastise me. He never did.

With shaking hands, I prepared the tripod and flask, and turned on the Bunsen burner underneath it. Slowly, I added the last ingredient to the mix in the flask.

Beside me, Claire grinned as she finished her potion. It was a bright, clear blue liquid, like the picture in the book.

"You did it!" I said, smiling at her. "Congrats!"

Red tinted her cheeks. "Thanks."

Seeing she had finished, Professor Crimson stopped by our desk. He took out a long silver spoon from his pocket and put it inside the flask. He stirred it once, twice, then lifted the spoon.

"It's a little thicker than it's supposed to be," he said. "Do it again."

Claire's shoulder deflated and her jaw slackened. Clueless to his daughter, Professor Crimson walked away, stopped by another student's desk, criticized his work too, and moved on. Still, Claire didn't say anything. She didn't even move.

"Don't listen to him," I whispered to her. "Your potion looks perfect."

"But he doesn't think so," she muttered. "If I don't do it again, he'll enter a bad grade for the day."

"You can talk to Professor Wesley afterward and explain," I said. "I'm sure he'll understand."

Shaking her head, Claire dragged her feet to the shelves in the back of the room, to gather more ingredients.

What a freaking clown Professor Crimson was. Why was he so hard on his own daughter when she was the best student in the entire academy? Though she might not be great at martial arts, she knew the theory and got As in her other classes. If she were my daughter, I would be damn proud of her.

Fury and frustration boiled in my blood.

Holding the ingredients, Claire came back to our desk. "Just forget about it," she said, dropping the ingredients on the desk. "Finish your potion before it's too late." I closed my hands into fists. If only I could slap some sense into him ... Claire nudged me with her elbow. "Erin, I'm serious. Just focus on your work."

Professor Crimson changed rows and was approaching from the other side. Shit, she was right. He would soon be by my side, and I would never hear the end of it if I wasn't at least close to finishing the damn potion.

I rolled my shoulders, trying to expel some of my pent-up feelings from my muscles, and added a bit more rosemary to my mixture.

The liquid, which was clear until then, started turning green.

Claire eyed my flask. "What did you add?"

"Rosemary," I said. I pointed to the little petri dish beside the tripod.

She brought it to her nose. "No, this is something else." She picked up another petri dish that was on the other side of the table and sniffed it. "This is tarragon."

"Oh shit," I muttered. Tarragon wasn't even on the list.

The green liquid started bubbling.

Professor Crimson yelled, "Stand back!"

But it was too late.

My flask exploded, sending the wrong potion mixture and glass everywhere. The other students had ducked behind their desks, and I had turned my back to it.

When it was over, I turned back. The green potion was a

goo on the desk and the lab instruments. It had gotten on my jacket and burned a hole through it, but thankfully, it hadn't gone deep and gotten on my skin.

"Oh, no," Claire whispered beside me.

I turned to her, and horror washed over me. The green liquid had splattered all over her. Her clothes, her hair, her hands, her face. Holes appeared in her clothes and ugly red marks spread over her skin.

"No, no, no," I chanted, reaching for her.

"Don't touch me!" she yelled, taking a step back. She groaned, and from the tears in her eyes, I was sure it was hurting like hell.

"Erin, take Claire to the infirmary immediately!" Professor Crimson said, his voice even colder and harsher than before. "Then report to my office."

That meant I was doomed, but I didn't care. He could expel me from the academy and I wouldn't care right now. All I cared about was helping Claire.

Under everyone's curious and scolding gazes, I ushered her out of the classroom. I wanted to hold on to her and pull her faster, but she kept yelling at me to not touch her.

Tears brimmed in my eyes when we finally arrived at the infirmary. Claire stepped inside and immediately fainted. Not caring about getting burned, I wrapped my arms around her and tried to hold on to her, but she was just as heavy as I was.

"Help!" I screamed as we both went down. At least, I broke her fall.

A woman in a white lab coat rushed to us. Two other people showed up. They took Claire through the foyer while I stayed sprawled on the floor, unable to move.

If I answered any of the questions, I didn't remember. At that moment, I felt numb and mute. It was like watching my aunt stepping in the way of the demon and being killed all over again.

Because of me, my aunt was dead.

Because of me, Claire was hurt.

One of the physicians approached me and asked a zillion questions. "What happened? What was in the potion? Did she ingest it? Are you hurt?"

I was taken to another stretcher across the room, where the physician cleaned a burn on the top of my hand. It seemed I had gotten a little of the potion on my skin when I touched Claire.

From here, I watched as they worked on a fainted Claire. They cut off most of her clothes, cleaned the wounds, and injected something in her.

Guilt squeezed my insides, making me out of breath.

"Erin," the physician called me. I turned my eyes to her. "You weren't badly burned. Keep applying this cream and the wound will go away soon." She put the cream tube in my hands. "You should go now. Go to your dorm, take the rest of the day off. I'll write a note and let your professors know. You won't be penalized for missing your classes."

What about Claire? Would I be penalized for hurting the only friend I had made so far?

I wanted to ask her how Claire was. If her burns had been severe, if she would have any permanent marks, if she would be okay.

My heart squeezed. They didn't seem desperate, so I didn't think her life was in danger, but with burn marks, there wasn't much the doctors could do. If she had been severely burned, then it could go either way.

The physician grabbed my arm and dragged me back to the foyer. I was so numb, she had to push me out the door.

I stood in front of the Daffodil building, the warm late morning sun shining down on me, the beautiful and eerie Blackthorn tree in front of me. A tear rolled down my cheek. My insides hurt with guilt and sorrow.

This was too much. On top of all the other bad things happening, I also hurt my best friend. Obviously, this demon hunter life wasn't for me. I wasn't sure why I had ever believed I could do this.

Determined, I went to my room and packed a small bag with some clothes, toiletries, a little money, and a picture of my aunt and me. I looked around, at all the things I would leave behind, including my aunt's Dawnblade. It was okay. I couldn't carry it all with me and I wasn't even sure I wanted them. Everything here would just remind me of how I had killed my aunt, or hurt Claire.

I checked my phone—we couldn't use it around the campus and the internet in here was limited, but I downloaded a map of the region, so if I got lost, I could count on it.

I changed into my workout clothes, slung my backpack across my shoulders, and went to the back of the Hyacinth building. Thankfully, all the other students were in class and I didn't see anyone in my way. Professor Crimson was probably waiting for me in his office; he could wait for me forever.

A few yards from the Hyacinth building and the running track was the back outer wall and the guard outpost. I swallowed hard and approached it.

"What are you doing here?" one of the guards asked.

"I'm going for a run," I lied. I had heard there were two trails outside the walls for students to walk or run. Usually, only fourth-year students were allowed to do that under a professor's supervision, but I had a trick up my sleeve. I pulled out the paper from my pocket and waved it in his face, so he couldn't read it right. "I have a pass from Professor Martha." I pointed to her signature. "If you don't let me go out, you'll have to talk to her."

The guard's eyes widened. Professor Martha's reputation only fell short of Professor Crimson's, and I was really counting on this. The guard turned to another one, who waved it off.

"All right," the guard said, opening the small gate beside the outpost. "You have an hour."

Or what? Would he come after me? I really doubted that.

"Thanks," I said as I walked past the back wall.

The gate clicked closed behind me and I inhaled deeply. I was free and alone, and I couldn't hurt anyone else.

I didn't waste time. I picked the longest trail and started running. But, as soon as the trees closed around it, I veered off the trail and followed the map, hoping it was right. I ran west, to the nearest town.

One good thing came from this past month of hard training: My resistance and stamina had increased tenfold. I now could endure running for much longer.

But I wasn't invincible. After an hour running, the pain shooting up my legs was too much. I slowed down to a brisk walk, but I didn't stop. I didn't dare stop. I wanted to put distance between the academy and me. I wanted to put this chapter of my life behind me and start over, far away from here.

What I would do, where I would go, I didn't know. All that mattered was becoming someone new.

It took me a few hours, but I finally arrived at West Hill, the nearest small town. There, I changed into normal clothes —jeans and tee—in a bus station's bathroom, then caught the bus to Liberty Creek. It had been the last place I had been with Rey before he whisked me to the academy, but it was a bigger town, from where I could get a train out of the state.

In Liberty Creek, the bus station was only a few blocks from the train station, so I walked there. The moon hung high in the sky. It was getting awfully late, but I was hoping to get a train that was leaving right away, and I would sleep on the way to wherever.

Walking through the streets, I saw a pub open. My stomach growled. I halted and considered stopping for a few minutes, just to grab something to eat, but the thought of missing the last train and having to sleep in town poked in my mind. Reluctantly, I marched on.

"Erin?" a voice called me.

Rigid, I turned around. The werewolf Wyatt was at the pub's door. "Hey."

"It is you." He walked to me. "What are you doing here? How's the academy?"

I shrugged. "I don't think I belong there."

"But aren't you a demon hunter?"

"I think so, but it's okay. Just because I was born one doesn't mean I have to be one, right?"

"Right." He tilted his head. "So, where are you going?"

"I don't really know," I confessed. "I was heading to the train station. My plan is to get a ticket to the farthest place they have. Or any place as long as it leaves tonight."

Wyatt picked up his phone and glanced at the screen. "It's almost midnight. If they didn't change the schedule, the last train left about half an hour ago, and the next one will be at five in the morning."

I frowned. "How do you know that?"

"I wanted to get as far away as I could once."

"Gotcha," I said. I wouldn't ask him any question he didn't

want to answer, hoping he would reciprocate it. "So, know any motels or whatever where I can spend the night?"

"Actually, I was about to head home," he said. "If you want, you can stay at my place."

Rey had trusted him, so that meant I could trust him too, right? "Are you sure?"

"Of course." He beckoned me to follow him. "Come on. My car is parked that way."

We crossed the street and walked by a dark alley. A cold chill blew from the alley and the hairs on my arm stood on end.

Wyatt halted beside me, his nose wrinkled.

"What is it?" I asked in a low voice.

"There's something ..." He closed his eyes, and I believed he was using his wolf ears to listen. "Watch out!"

He grabbed my wrist and pulled me out of the way as a dark shadow lunged out of the alley.

I had to scramble not to fall, but once I was behind Wyatt, I took a good glance at the shadow.

Only it wasn't a shadow. It was a freaking Screinor. I had studied them earlier this month. They had long dark gray bodies slick with what looked like slime, huge mouths in a round shaped head, and no apparent eyes or ears.

"Erin, run!" Wyatt said, his voice thicker than before. I quickly realized why. He was shifting. In no time, his clothes ripped off and he stood in front of me, a big, light brown wolf. He growled at the demon.

More Screinors stepped out of the alley. I retreated, but they quickly surrounded us.

"It's you," one of them said, his voice a thin drawl. He pointed at me. "We want you."

I glanced at my wrist. The damn demon mark. It still

hadn't gone away. Rey had been telling the truth. This mark would really attract demons to me. Shit.

Wyatt let out a short howl, then jumped at the demon in front of him.

"No!" I said, as the demon let out a piercing shriek.

Wyatt fell to the ground writhing in pain as the shock from the demon's shriek spread through his body. Another demon leaned over him and shrieked again.

This time, Wyatt fainted.

And I was left alone with the demons.

12

––––––––

REY

I was between classes when I heard about Erin and Claire's accident in the potion-making class. Of course, by now it had become a string of rumors.

"Erin messed the potion up on purpose to hurt Claire."

"I heard Claire is dying."

"Claire deserved it."

"I hope Erin is expelled."

Hating the rumors, I rushed to the infirmary to check on Claire.

By the time I arrived, she was seated on a hospital bed, several bandages around her arms and hands, and one on her neck.

"How is she?" I asked Cecile, who was checking Claire's vitals.

"She's fine," Cecile said. "The burns weren't severe. With time and care, they will all go away."

That was a relief. I turned to Claire. "What happened?"

"It was nothing," Claire said, her voice low. "Erin was nervous because my father was the one teaching our class this morning. She got confused between two ingredients and the potion exploded."

"Was she hurt?" I asked.

"She had burns on her hands," Cecile answered. "She was shocked, though. I sent her to her room to rest, poor thing."

"She was supposed to meet my father in his office after class," Claire told me. "He was probably going to grill her about it."

Cecile groaned. "Between us, I hope she didn't go. He'd just make it worse."

I frowned, not liking where this was going. "Any ideas when Claire is going to be released?"

"I'm keeping her here tonight to see if any of the potion's ingredients will react within her," Cecile said. "At this point, I doubt anything will happen, but I would rather be thorough."

I nodded. "As you should." I glanced at Claire. "Enjoy your rest."

She frowned. "Rey, can you please check on Erin? I fainted and I'm worried she's upset."

I hesitated. "Sure. I will."

She offered me a small smile. "Thanks."

I nodded, then walked out of the Daffodil building.

I groaned. I had been thinking about Erin even before Claire asked me to check on her, but now the urgency of it hit me harder. If Claire had passed out, Erin might still be upset.

Fuck.

I had vowed to stay away from her, but here I was, walking to her dorm. I couldn't even lie to myself that I was going because Claire asked, or because, as the head of the security on campus, I wanted to make sure she wasn't hurt.

Me, the half-human, half-demon, screwed-up Rey, wanted to know if Erin was okay.

I ran inside the female dorm, raced up the stairs to the second floor, and knocked on the door of her room.

No answer. Was she sleeping?

"Erin," I called. "It's Rey. Open the door, please." No answer. I knocked again. "It's school business. I need to check if you're okay." Still no fucking answer.

I shouldn't use my powers here, but I couldn't help myself. I placed my hand on the door, closed my eyes, and sent my senses out. Sometimes my weak half-demon senses deceived me, but this time, I thought they were right.

Anxiety coursing through me, I grabbed the knob and tried to open her door. Locked, as I expected. But this wasn't enough to stop me. Sure I would regret this later, I used my demon strength and broke the knob.

The door swung open and I stepped in. She wasn't here. I checked the closet and the bathroom, but she wasn't here.

Where the hell could she be?

I walked out of the building, raking my brain. Erin didn't have any other friends, so there was no one else I could ask. I went to the library, where she spent a lot of time studying with Claire. Then, I stopped by the Hyacinth building, where she trained with Professor Martha during unholy hours.

I even walked the courtyard, knowing she liked to stroll through here after lunch, before going to her afternoon classes.

It seemed I knew a fucking lot about her, except where to find her.

I was on my way to Professor Martha's office when I spotted her marching toward me.

"I was looking for you," she told me, her voice with a little more pitch than normal. She halted in front of me, and I realized she was breathing hard. "I believe Erin ran away."

"What?" I shook my head, confused. "How?"

"She tricked the guards at the northeast outpost." Professor Martha explained Erin had used her permission slip to go out for a run on the back trails, but that was several hours ago. The guards went after her, but couldn't find her. After realizing they had been deceived, they reported Erin missing. "I need you to find her immediately."

I frowned. If Randall found out, he would have my skin. Moreover, the thought of Erin out there alone, while demons swarmed every corner of this world ... it terrified me.

"I'm on it." I nodded once. "Just keep Randall from finding out while I'm gone, otherwise the three of us will be in trouble."

She groaned. "I know. I'll do what I can."

I spun around and ran to Erin's room where I got one of her pens from her desk, then ran toward the underground garage for my car, and headed out of the academy.

A mile out, I stopped. Going out without direction was a waste of time, so I pulled out the pen I had gotten from Erin's room, and tried mimicking a tracking spell I had learned from a witch long ago. My demon powers were much different from hers, but I hoped the spell worked anyway.

It was a crude spell, but I felt it, the tug inside my chest, as if there was a line tied between Erin and me, and it kept pulling and getting shorter. As fast as I could, I followed it.

Erin had gotten farther than I expected. Following the pull, I drove to Liberty Creek. The tug was getting stronger, as if the cord was shorter and would snap at any moment.

I drove by the bus station, and finally, the pull ceased.

I hit the brakes. The car stopped and a few feet ahead I saw them. A dozen or so Screinors.

All of them surrounding Erin.

Rage blinded me.

I jumped out of the car and summoned my Dawnblade.

A few of the demons noticed me coming and turned, ready to shriek my senses away. Hoping Erin was busy staying alive, I used my demon magic and created an invisible shield in front of me, which bounced back their shriek, dizzying them instead.

Taking advantage of their momentary confusion and pain, I slashed them down with my blade. I stepped into the circle as Erin dodged the claws of a demon, just to fall into the hands of another. He wrapped his ugly arms around her and shrieked in her ear.

Erin tried clamping her ears, but the demon didn't let her. What the fuck? I brought my blade down on this back. Dizzy, Erin stumbled back. I wound my arm around her waist and pulled her to me.

"Erin, stay awake," I urged her. Sometimes, when the victim of the Screinors fainted, they could wake up confused. Some even lost their memories.

She blinked. "It hurts."

"Just hang on," I muttered.

A demon lunged at us, and I took a step back, with Erin glued to my side. The demon opened his mouth to shriek, but I reached forward and brought my sword down on his ugly face.

Then another one shrieked.

Once again, I used magic to stop it. I dropped Erin beside Wyatt—what was that naked werewolf doing here?—and advanced on the demons, still disoriented from their own scream. I finished them up.

I glanced around.

What a fucking mess.

Several demon bodies, a dazed demon hunter, and a passed out werewolf in his birthday suit. At least, there weren't any humans around to witness it.

I made a quick call to have a lesser demon under Asmodeus's command come clean this up. I picked up Erin in my arms and loaded her into my car. Then, I grabbed one of my bigger jackets from the trunk—a demon hunter on the road always had his trunk full of everything he might need—placed it over Wyatt's naked body, and poked his back with the tip of my boot.

"Wake up."

The werewolf stirred for a moment, but soon regained his senses and sat up with a start. "What happened?"

"Since your clothes are gone, I'm assuming you shifted, and when the demons knocked you out, you turned back into a human."

He shook his head, probably still a little dazed. If he had been a normal human, he wouldn't have woken up for hours, but since Wyatt had werewolf genes, his healing powers and his metabolism processed it all faster. His eyes went wide. "Where's Erin?"

"In my car." I pointed to my jacket barely covering his body. I would have to burn the thing afterward. "Put that on, and let's go."

I didn't wait for him. I turned and went back to my car. I sat behind the wheel and glanced at Erin. We needed to get out of here before she attracted more demons.

Wearing my coat, Wyatt approached the car. I lowered the window to talk to him. "Aren't you coming with us?" I asked.

"My car is right there." He pointed to his car of the week. Since they were all stolen, he switched it every few weeks.

"I need to take Erin someplace so she can rest." I didn't want to take her to the academy like this. "Any ideas?"

Wyatt nodded. "My place. Follow me."

He jogged to his car—a beat-up truck—and peeled out over the curb. I started the engine of my car and followed him through the streets of Liberty Creek.

I tried resisting, but I ended up stealing more glances at Erin. Her long, black hair was a curtain over her face, and her head lolled back, as if she was drunk. She brought her hand up to her head, and I saw the mark on her wrist. Yeah, I was sure she had been the one who attracted those fucking demons.

An immense sense of relief hit me hard in the chest. Holy fuck, so many bad things could have happened to her, but she was fine. I had gotten to her in time, and she was fine now.

"What's going on?" she asked, her voice slurred as she fought against the vertigo. "Where are you taking me?"

"Just relax," I told her. "Whatever you're feeling will pass in a few minutes."

She groaned but relented.

Ten minutes later, Wyatt pulled his truck into the parking lot of an abandoned building on the town's outskirts. He parked the car and gestured for us to follow him inside.

I helped Erin out of my car, but by now, she was already less wobbly. Even so, I stayed by her side, my arms ready to catch her should she stumble.

Inside the building, we headed to the back, to a thin metal door in the back. Wyatt unlocked all three hundred locks securing the doors, then pushed them open. A wide and rough concrete staircase greeted us.

"My place is upstairs," he said, climbing up the steps.

This time, I grabbed Erin's wrist and helped her up the stairs. I was expecting her to bitch about it, but she didn't. In fact, by the middle of the staircase, she had grabbed my arm with her other hand.

The staircase opened to a huge loft. It was crude, but at the same time, inviting. A wide area with a huge, velvet sectional, the biggest flat TV I had ever seen, an island with five metal stools in a kitchen with outdated appliances, and in the far back, a king bed in front of a wall of glass that overlooked a wide valley. Right now, in the middle of the night, I could only see a few twinkling lights and the stars in the sky, but I bet that during the day, it was a breathtaking view.

"I thought you said your place was small and messy," I said, narrowing my eyes at our host.

He shrugged as if that was a good excuse.

I helped Erin to the sectional, then faced Wyatt again.

He pointed to a door in the back of the loft. "I'm going to take a shower and put on some clothes. Make yourselves at home. There should be some drinks and food in the fridge."

"Thanks," I replied.

He disappeared in what I assumed was the bathroom.

Erin groaned. "I want some water." She started getting up from the couch, but I gently pushed her down again.

"I'll get it for you." I went to the kitchen and found bottles of water in the fridge. I grabbed one and handed it to Erin.

She thanked me, then took a big swallow of water.

By now, the effect of the demon's shriek should be almost over. Those fucking demons ... Once more I thought about all the shitty things that could have happened to her, and the relief I felt seconds ago disappeared, quickly replaced by rage and frustration.

"What the fuck were you thinking?" I practically shouted. Erin's eyes rounded, startled by my outburst. I went on, "I told you it wasn't safe for you outside the academy. Did you really think you could make it alone out here? Or did you think I was joking?"

Lowering her gaze, she dropped the water bottle on the side table. "I wasn't thinking." She returned her pretty golden eyes to me, so full of sorrow. "I don't belong there. Even if I am a demon hunter, that's not my place in this world. I can't go back."

I clenched my fists. "You have to."

"No, I don't," she said, serious. "Nobody can keep me there against my will."

At a loss for words, I sat down on the corner of the sectional and turned to her, my knees touching hers. "Don't you want to live?" She didn't answer, but she didn't break my stare either. I reached for her arm and turned her wrist around. "That mark will attract demons to you. And if it weren't for that, it's like demons can sense demon hunters. That alone is a permanent target on your back. Forever. You can't run from that."

"I don't belong there," she repeated, her voice low.

"Why do you say that?"

She scoffed. "Where to start? I'm terrible at martial arts, I can't seem to wrap my head around demon history, and let's not talk about potion making and how I almost killed Claire."

"Claire is fine," I told her.

Her breath caught. "Really?"

I nodded. "Yes. The burns weren't severe, and with the

magical healing creams our physicians have, they will be gone as if she was never burned."

A long sigh of relief escaped her lips. "Oh, thank goodness. I was so worried she would be scarred for life."

"She'll spend the night in the infirmary today, just for precaution, but tomorrow she should return to her normal activities," I told her, sounding like a fucking professor. I cleared my throat. "I bet she'll want to see you."

Erin shook her head, her long hair barely moving. "It's better if I'm away from there, from everyone."

I groaned on the inside. The last thing I wanted was to sound angered and make her afraid of me, of going back. "That's not true. As a demon hunter, you are the academy's responsibility. If you're attacked outside the campus, then they will have to do something about it."

Her delicate brows curled down. "I don't get it. Not all students finish their training. Not everyone turns into a full-fledged Blackthorn hunter."

"That's true, but most of those who don't become hunters either stay at the academy, or they work nearby, in a town just for them."

"What do you mean?"

The corners of my lips turned up. I kept forgetting she still didn't know much about demon hunters and the academy and everything else involved in it. "Are you tired? I hope you're not." I stood up and offered my hand. "Let's go. I have something to show you."

* * *

After yelling at Wyatt that we were leaving, I drove us out of town, toward the academy.

"I think you're taking me back to the academy," Erin said, sounding disappointed.

"Not yet. I promise." I glanced at her in the dark of the car, but I still could see the silhouette of her face and the little pout she had.

"Not yet, you just said."

I tried not to smile. "After I show you this, you'll want to go back."

She crossed her arms and turned to me. "Is that a bet?"

This time, I smiled. "It can be. What do you want to bet?"

"Shit, let me think on it."

I chuckled.

Five miles from the academy, I veered onto another road, drove for another five miles, until we arrived in a small village at the base of the mountain.

It was past four in the morning, but the village was still awake, with twinkling white lights spread around the charming stone streets, flanked by beige and brown houses, pubs, shops, and homey restaurants.

People with their phones out milled the streets, taking pictures left and right, talking, laughing, entering the shops, leaving the restaurants ...

I parked the car in a spot on the street and hopped out. On the other side, Erin got out of the car, her eyes wide and her mouth open, as she looked around at the place.

"What is this place?" she asked when I halted by her side.

"This is Chasseur Ville. It's a town the hunters created centuries ago. Most demon hunters who don't join the Blackthorn hunters full-fledged group come to live here. Each family, or hunter, has a house and a business." I gestured around us. "But these people you see are all humans."

"Why are they here?"

"Chasseur Ville was created to be a tourist town." I tugged at her sleeve and we strolled down the sidewalk. "The humans come here, to this hidden gem, and spend their money, thus providing for the demon hunters who didn't make the cut."

"But you just told me it's not safe for a hunter to be outside the academy."

"This place is an extension of the academy. It's protected the same way; you just can't see it. Moreover, even though these hunters didn't join the main group, most of them were trained. They can defend themselves, and each other, if demons show up."

Which made me think. Why were demons breaking into the academy and not here?

"How have I never heard of this place?" Erin asked, bringing my thoughts back to the here and now. "It's so close to where I was raised. I should have heard about it."

I shook my head as a group of humans hurried past us. "Let's just say this is a hidden treasure. This place is not advertised; it's discovered."

Another group ran past us. Erin watched them, curious. "But how?"

"I could tell you—" I leaned in closer to her and whispered, "But then I would have to kill you."

She shot me a glare. "I'm serious." An animated group exited the restaurant behind us, and while chatting happily, they crossed the street and went into a jewelry store. "Okay, what's going on? Everyone seems so busy."

"It's a treasure hunt."

"What?"

Despite myself, I was enjoying how confused she was. "The tourists who come here are handed a map and a clue. From there, it's a treasure hunt."

"And what's the prize?"

"A free stay at the castle." I pointed down the road, where the castle was located. Because it was dark, we could only make out the light coming from a few windows. "It's approximately the size of the academy's Aster building, but it's really fancy, and not open to the public. Only the winners of the treasure hunt can stay there."

"What if there are too many winners?"

"That never happens," I told her. "The hunt is too hard."

"A hunt organized by hunters." She scoffed. "That's quite amusing."

I surprised even myself with my next words. "Want to try?"

Erin narrowed her golden eyes at me. "I'm not good with those. I think I would rather walk around and see what all the fuss is about."

"I'm okay with that."

First, I took her to a diner with the most wonderful pancakes I had ever eaten. Erin was shocked when I greeted everyone by their names. What did she expect? The demon hunter community wasn't large, and since I was "the chosen one"—as some people liked to call me, because Randall favored me—I knew everyone.

As I expected, Erin loved the pancakes. What I didn't expect was to have my stomach tighten every time she took a bite and moaned. Holy fuck ...

Next, I took her to a series of small shops: perfumes,

jewelry, watches, house goods, makeup, clothing—all handmade.

In the perfume shop, she tried one on. Without thinking, I grabbed it from her and put it down.

"Hey, I was going to try that," she argued.

"You don't need perfume," I said.

"What do you mean?"

I stared into her bright eyes. "The one you're using is already perfect."

Her cheeks tinted red.

Heat spread through my core. I lowered my gaze and exited the shop.

From there, we went to the biggest and most popular shop in Chasseur Ville—the Noir Coin.

"The Black Corner. That is a curious name," she said as she entered the store.

Every nook and cranny was crammed with small boxes, flasks, crystal balls, crystal shards, herbal bags, and more.

"Everything here is magical," I told her.

Once more, she looked at me with huge eyes. "For real?"

"In some way." I picked up a flask with a label that read *Love Potion*. "If I were to give you this, you would think highly of me, maybe be infatuated for a day or two, but not really love me."

"I already think highly of you," she blurted out. Her cheeks reddened again. "I mean ... you know what I mean!"

No, I didn't, but that piqued my interest. She thought highly of me? Why? What had I done to deserve her esteem? I had been cold to her, pushed her away from me since we arrived at the academy.

"The trinkets and potions in here are enchanted, but it's only superficially, and not meant to last," I told her, trying to keep the ball rolling so she wouldn't hide from me. "Humans love everything in here. It's where they spend most of their money when they visit Chasseur Ville."

She looked around, her hands hovering over the trinkets. "I can see why."

I watched as she grabbed a ring with a huge crystal setting. The crystal was supposed to change colors, just like those silly mood rings, but this one was for warnings. Pink meant a loved one was close. Blue meant something good was about to happen. Red meant something bad. Black meant death.

My gut tensed when the crystal in Erin's hand turned red. "What does red mean?" she muttered, reaching for the label on the shelf.

"That you're loved," I spat out, improvising. I took her hand and slipped the ring off her finger. "Come on. There's one more place I want to show you."

The Noir Coin was across the street from the castle gates.

Erin eyed the closed gates. "I thought only the winners of the treasure hunt could stay there."

"True, but I know the guards. We can peek inside."

As I thought, I knew the guards on gate duty and they didn't object to me taking Erin on a tour of the castle.

The castle was like any other on the outside—tall, a stone façade, with long windows, and a couple of towers. Inside, it looked like the most impressive mansion on this side of the world. The foyer had marble floors and crystal chandeliers, a winding staircase, and windows, and there were too many rooms to count inside: a drawing room, a game room, a music room, three sitting rooms, two dining rooms, three studies, a gym, an Olympic-sized indoor pool, a huge library, and eight guest suites.

I took Erin to the balcony atop the tallest tower of the castle when I finished the tour. For a moment, I felt distressed there, thinking of Brianne, who had committed suicide by jumping off a similar balcony at the academy. That case had been so weird. After no clues were found, it had been ruled a suicide. That hadn't rubbed well with me, but I had been so busy going to classes, doing all the other tasks Randall asked of me, and overseeing the campus's security, I had already forgotten about it.

I thought of myself as a bad guy. My half-demon side was dominant, and there was nothing I could do to fight it. Yet, I didn't like seeing senseless death.

"This is incredible," Erin whispered, leaning over the iron rail to look at the village below.

An urge to hold on to her, to make sure she wouldn't slip and fall, hit me. I was being ridiculous. Shaking my head to expel those thoughts, I leaned on the rail beside her. "Isn't it?"

I never took much time to appreciate the little things in life, not after my contract with Asmodeus and an eternity of demon servitude, but at the moment, I was glad I was here with Erin. The village stretched below us, a faint silhouette in the night, framed by the bright white twinkling lights illuminating the streets.

Above us, billions of stars dotted the sky, and a crescent moon shone atop the mountain behind us.

"This place is magical." She smiled at me. "Thank you for bringing me here."

I stared into her eyes and became easily lost in them. I had realized she was a pretty girl the first moment I saw her at that haunted house, but the more time I spent with her, the more I saw her, the more beautiful she became.

Perhaps it was this place working its magic in my dead

chest, or perhaps it really was because I had never laid eyes on a more beautiful young woman before.

I wasn't sure. All I knew was that I wanted to lean into her. I wanted to wrap my arms around her and pull her to me. I wanted to kiss her.

Shocked, I took a step back. "You're welcome." I ran a hand through my hair, trying to control my feelings and thoughts. Misdirection. Distraction. I cleared my throat. "So, are you convinced demon hunters are cool yet?"

She shot me a fake-glare. "Cool as in, wow, they have a secret town and are tricking humans kind of cool?"

"You know what I mean." I leaned back on the rail, but this time not so close to her. "Even if you fail your classes and don't become a full-fledged hunter, I'm showing you that you have a place to go after. A cool, magical place. If you want, of course."

She frowned. "Are they forced to come here? I mean, if they fail, are they forced to either work at the academy or move here?"

"No, not at all," I said. "Demon hunters can leave, but most that leave die, or spend so much time fighting demons, that they come back." And with that mark, one day wouldn't go by without demons knocking on her door. If only I could make her understand that.

"Okay," she whispered.

"Okay?"

"I'll go back to the academy with you."

I gaped at her. "Just like that? I thought I would have to grill you."

She shrugged. "Like you said, I'm in danger out here alone. I can try leaving again, once I finish at the academy and can defend myself." She turned her arm around and glanced down to her wrist. "When this mark is off my wrist."

"You're making the right decision," I told her. A wave of relief coursed through me. Yes, she was going back with me. She would be safe. That was all that mattered right now. I nudged her with my elbow. "All right, the sun is almost up. We'd better get back."

She glanced at the village once more, then to the sky. The shine of the moon bathed her fair skin, her pink lips, her long neck. I felt myself reaching for her, wanting to run my fingers along her throat.

She turned to me, clueless of my desire, and smiled at me. "All right. Let's go."

13

ERIN

ONCE I WAS BACK AT THE ACADEMY, I HAD TO SIT THROUGH several lectures. One from Professor Martha, who I thought would hit me while she yelled at me. A second one from Claire, who promised she wasn't mad at me and knew it was an accident. She made me promise I wouldn't run away again. And lastly from Headmaster Randall. I had seen him around campus a few times, but this meeting was my first time talking to him. Like Martha, Randall said he was disappointed in me—only in a much lower voice, but no less intimidating. He went on to say that I had put not only myself in danger, but jeopardized the safety of the entire campus, and that I would have some kind of punishment.

I dreaded that, but my punishment wasn't too bad. Instead of waking up at five to train with Professor Martha, I now had to wake up at four and run—inside the campus's walls.

The first week was brutal. The second not so much. By the fourth week, I was noticing my resistance and stamina improving.

Rey had returned to his quiet and cold self. After showing me a magical time, telling me that my perfume was perfect, telling me that I was pretty, and then confessing he had broken the doorknob to my dorm room because he had been worried about me—something that had already been fixed—he practically disappeared. Now, I only saw him in our weapon forging class, and even then, he only spoke to me about class-related subjects. My heart broke a little because of it. I thought we had shared a moment, a connection, and I was sad to see it had just been me.

One thing that hadn't changed, though, was Ava and her friends, Stella and Ruby. They were still as mean and hateful as usual. Ava's new hobby was to tease me about running away. She kept saying she had kicked my ass so much, I had decided to quit. Well, it wasn't entirely wrong, but that had been one thing among thirty others.

I did my best to ignore her, though.

One sunny afternoon, Claire and I went to our monster identification class.

Harvey, the star student—after Claire—was always in a bad mood during this class, since his mother, Professor Eleanor, was the teacher. Claire told me she had been an amazing demon hunter, the best one of the Blackthorn hunters, but she had gotten injured during a hunt, and now she couldn't hunt anymore.

"Open your book to chapter twelve," Professor Eleanor said. She sat at the edge of her desk, her book in hand. "Today, we'll talk about vampires."

Whispers spread through the class.

"What is it?" I asked Claire.

"It's said she killed an entire coven by herself," Claire whispered to me.

"Silence!" Professor Eleanor snapped. "I know what you're talking about. About my solo hunt." She embraced her book. "Yes, I went out to hunt vampires by myself and was able to eliminate an entire coven. Vampires, like any other supernatural species, like any demon, are evil and must be killed." She opened her book. "Who can describe what vampires look like?" Claire raised her hand. Professor Eleanor didn't even look up when she said, "Yes, Claire?"

"They look like humans, but all of them are beautiful," Claire answered. During classes that required physical strength, she hid in the back, but during the other classes, she was always the first to speak up. "It's part of their trick. They attract humans with their stunning good looks. When hungry, or angry, their fangs come out."

Professor Eleanor nodded. "Because they don't have visible traits other than beauty, it's hard to identify them. Same goes for werewolves, when they aren't shapeshifted."

I frowned, thinking of what the professor said. "So," I started, surprising myself, "werewolves are evil too?"

"All supernaturals are evil," Professor Eleanor barked. "In some ways, werewolves are worse than vampires because they have short tempers. And, when young, most can't control their shift and bloodlust under the full moon, making them unstable." She shook her head once. "All supernaturals are evil. Know that. Live by that."

But ... how could she be right about that? Wyatt was a werewolf, and he had been nice to me. And he was Rey's friend, Rey who was a demon hunter like me. It didn't make sense.

I kept quiet the rest of the class so I wouldn't be yelled at again.

I was glad when we were dismissed. Before all the

students filed out of the classroom, Professor Eleanor approached Harvey's desk.

"Why didn't you raise your hand and answered my questions?" she asked, her tone sharp. "Not even once."

I picked up my things and nudged Claire, who was still writing notes, to go. I didn't want to hear whatever they were going to talk about.

"I didn't want to," Harvey said, his voice unusually serious. From the corner of my eyes, I saw him leaned back in his chair, as if he didn't have a care in the world. "All of this is bullshit."

His mother slapped her hand on his desk. It startled me and I pushed on Claire for us to go. Now!

"You disappoint me," Professor Eleanor said. Didn't she realize there were still a few students in the classroom? She didn't care we could hear her? "You disappoint your father. He's an amazing demon hunter, and if you keep up with this —" She gestured to him. "—attitude, you'll never live up to his legacy."

"Who says I want to?"

"Harvey Walton!" she yelled. I grabbed Claire's arm and pulled her out of the room, but not before I could hear the rest of Professor Eleanor's sentence. "Keep that up and I'll disown you. I'll cut you off and you'll have nothing." Heavy footsteps followed and I assumed she was stomping out of the classroom.

"Go, go, go," I urged Claire.

From there, we went to the library for our free period. I still had plenty of studying to do in last year's subjects, and Claire never passed on the opportunity to check her homework—for the tenth time.

Ava and her snob friends were also in the library,

pretending to study as usual. She kept firing me glances and whispering, probably trying to irritate me. She would be disappointed to find out I really didn't care what she thought of me. Was she going to tease me about running away for the rest of my life? Who cared?

A few minutes later, Harvey and Peter strolled into the library. Harvey had his usual half-smile on, his shoulders relaxed, and his walk with an I-know-I'm-hot gait. All the girls on campus swooned over him. Well, I had to admit he was cute with his toned skin, brown eyes, and short dark brown hair. He was tall and well-built too, with plenty of muscles—I had seen his arms and shoulders during martial arts class.

But, Harvey never dated anyone. He flirted with all the girls at the academy, including me. Like right now. He and Peter sat down at the table directly in front of mine, and he kept smiling and staring at me.

"I think he likes you," Claire whispered to me.

"That's just Harvey being Harvey," I whispered back. "He does that to all the girls."

"He has been like that for over a month already," she said. "Usually, when the girl doesn't give him the time of day, which is rare, he moves on. He still hasn't moved on."

I tsked. "It's just because I'm the new girl. He's probably getting a kick out of that."

Right? I glanced at him and sure enough, he had his cocky half-grin on and his eyes on me.

Self-conscious, I tucked a strand of my hair behind my ear and looked down at my book. I had to focus on this freaking war and learn the names of all the important figures, or I wouldn't understand the one we were reviewing now in demon history, and I would certainly fail the class.

But a thought poked at the back of my mind, and I looked up at Harvey again. Why was he flirting with me? He had so many other girls to flirt with. I was the oddball, the runaway girl, the one who was always getting into trouble because of her poor performance. The only reason why a star student like him would flirt with me was to play with me.

I shook my head and turned my eyes to my books.

The chair beside mine was pulled back and Ava sat down on it. "Whatever you're doing, just stop."

I frowned at her. "What the hell are you talking about?"

"You batting your eyelashes at Harvey," she said, her face serious. "Just stop."

"Why would I?" I indulged her, as if I really had been paying any attention to Harvey.

"You're new so you might not know this, but Harvey and I have been an item since birth," she told me, sounding proud of the fact. "Our parents were best friends and promised Harvey and I would get married one day. So, don't get your hopes up. You have no chance with him."

Until then, I hadn't taken Harvey's flirtations seriously, and I had no intention of reciprocating. But now ... now, I could see the thought of me irritating Ava by flirting with Harvey gave me pleasure.

"He's the one coming at me," I said, exaggerating a bit. "I don't think he got the memo about your impending wedding. Maybe you should talk to him about it."

Ava glared at me. "I'm warning you, Erin. He's mine. Stay away from him, or else."

She shot up and stalked away. At the other table, Harvey didn't move or react. He still stole glances at me, as if Ava had never been here.

"Wow," Claire muttered beside me.

"Did you know about that?" I asked her. "That they are promised to be married?"

"Yes, everyone knows," she told me. "But it's not like old times when the promise was a contract. It was more like a verbal agreement. Although, I think her family and his family still act like it's going to happen."

"It seems she thinks so too."

Honestly, I wasn't going to lose sleep over it. If Harvey really came on to me, I would consider giving him the time of day. I mean, I was single, right? The guy I thought I could have something with didn't even look my way, and irritating Ava in the process would be a bonus.

I resumed my studying, though it was only half-assed. My mind spun through what life would have been if I had been born in the midst of this world like they had. Would I have avoided Ava? Would I be like her? Would I have dated Harvey? Would I be a badass ninja who kicked everyone's ass in class?

I would never know.

About an hour later, I grew tired of studying and invited Claire to go with me to either the cafeteria to grab a snack, or the game room—a large hall on the first floor of the dorm building with big sofas, video games, arcade games, foosball and pool tables, and more. Claire said she wanted to finish up something, then she would meet me before our next class.

Not sure what I would do around campus without her, I walked out of the library.

"Erin," someone called me. I turned back to the Iris building entrance and saw Harvey walking toward me. "Hey." He halted before me. "I wanted to talk to you."

Holy shit. Was this Harvey coming on to me?

"Hm, yes?"

"I was going to the movie room with the guys and—"

"Movie room?" I asked, confused.

His sly grin stretched over his lips. Okay, I knew he was flirting right now, playing with me, probably to spite Ava, which I was okay with, but I had to admit that he was a little more than just cute. Seeing him up close, I noticed the warmth in his chocolate eyes, and the angles of his face. All right, he was handsome.

"Oh, damn, you wouldn't know." He put his hands in his pockets. "Every year, we find an empty room and turn it into a movie room. We bring in armchairs, inflatable sofas, and lots of pillows, a popcorn machine, a projector, and a sound system. We watch movies, usually late at night."

"That sounds ... interesting."

"The guys bought a new martial arts movie that is supposed to be super badass. I thought we could watch it together."

"Right now?"

"Yes." Harvey nodded. "Wanna come?"

"What's going on?"

I froze at the new voice.

Rey stepped to my side and faced Harvey, his gray eyes narrowed.

"Nothing you should concern yourself about," Harvey said, his entire demeanor changing. He straightened his back and puffed out his chest.

"I doubt that." Rey's mien also hardened. The two guys stared at each other, and I got the gist that there was a big beef between them. I would have to ask Claire if she knew anything about that.

"If you'll excuse us, Erin and I were leaving." Harvey reached for my arm.

Rey slapped his hand away. "The fuck you are." He wrapped his fingers around my wrist and tugged me closer. He looked down at my arm. "What the fuck?" He rubbed his finger over the demon mark. "This is still here?"

"Yeah," I said, jerking my arm free.

"It should have come off already." His brows slammed down. "You need to come with me."

14

Harvey protested, but Erin knew I wasn't kidding. She let me take her back into the library, to a restricted section in the back. This area was like the rest of the library, with tall shelves and lots of books, desks and chairs, but only professors and other assigned people had access to it.

I locked the door and turned to the side of the room with books about demons.

"What are we looking for?" Erin asked, following me.

"I want to know more about the demon who left that mark on you." I picked a book with a list of demons by ranking. "That mark should have faded several weeks ago." I grabbed several other books and took them all to the closest table. I pushed a couple to Erin. "Sit down and help me. Try to find something that resembles the mark on your wrist."

She narrowed her eyes at me. I knew what was probably going through her mind. After that night at Chasseur Ville, I became distant again. What else could I do? I had saved her from the other demons, but who would save her from me? I had to keep myself as far from her as I could.

This, however, felt important enough to put that plan on pause. This fucking mark had to be gone before it caused more trouble.

"Okay," she finally said, sitting down and turning the book to her.

For over an hour, Erin and I flipped through dozens, maybe hundreds of books. We found many marks and symbols, but none like the one on her wrist.

I slammed a book shut. "This is fucking ridiculous."

"Maybe this isn't anything to do with that demon," she said, eyes on the book she was flipping through.

"What do you mean?"

She shrugged. "I don't know. I'm just throwing ideas out there."

Ideas ... we needed ideas.

I stood up. "Come on."

She dropped the book and frowned at me. "Where to now?"

"Right here." I positioned myself in the middle of several desks. "I want you to try something." It was a crazy idea, but it was the only one I had right now.

Reluctantly, Erin rose from her spot and walked to me. I grabbed her shoulders and pushed her two feet in front of me. "All right, don't look at me like I'm crazy. Just turn your hand like this." I put my hand between us, palm up. Brows hitched high, Erin mimicked me. "Now, try to do some magic."

"What?"

"You're looking at me as if I'm crazy."

"Because that sounds completely crazy."

"Just ... indulge me."

She sighed. "And how do I do magic?"

How would I explain this to her without her realizing I was speaking from experience? "Focus on your energy. Imagine magic being something alive inside you, like your blood. Urge it to obey you, to follow your wishes, to come to your hand, to your palm, and create a fire ball."

"A fire ball?" She sounded more skeptical by the second.

"Please, Erin, just do this for me."

She rolled her eyes, but then stared at her open palm, as if she was focusing and following what I had told her. A moment later, the air around us crackled with tension.

Holy fuck ...

Magic shot out of her hand, creating a ball of darkfire.

I sucked in a sharp breath. Erin's eyes went wide, and she started screaming, shaking her hand rapidly to extinguish the black flames. I pressed my hand over her mouth, so no one would hear her scream, and grabbed her hand, making her close it in a tight fist.

The darkfire went out.

I helped Erin down to a chair and crouched before her.

"That was ... that was ..." She was shaking all over.

"That was magic, yes," I finished for her.

"If the other hunters find out I have magic, they will think I'm a supernatural," she muttered. "They will kill me." She recoiled, her eyes round. "You will kill me."

"No, no, I won't," I assured her. But she was right about the others. They would kill her on the spot. Unfortunately, there was more to it. "Erin, I have something to tell you." She turned her glassy eyes to me. "The kind of fire ball you created, it's darkfire. That is demon magic. For you to be able to use that kind of magic, you're either part demon, or you signed a contract with one." One that liked her too much and gave her powers to boot.

She shook her head. "I haven't made any contracts; I'm sure of it."

"Then I'm afraid to say that you're half-hunter and half-demon."

"No, no, no ..." Her breathing grew shallow.

Fuck, this girl would pass out on me and I would have to take her to the infirmary, something I really didn't want to do right now.

I went to the main part of the library, where a water fountain was located beside the front desk, grabbed a paper cup, filled it with water, and rushed back to Erin.

I handed the cup to her. "Here. Drink the water and take deep breaths." With shaking hands, Erin took the cup from me and almost spilled it as she brought it to her lips. She drank the water, then inhaled deeply. "One more time," I urged her.

Once more, she took a deep breath through her nose and let it out through her mouth. She repeated the action other two times.

"This can't be happening," she whispered, eyeing the empty paper cup. Her hands shook less and her breathing had calmed down. "I can't be half-demon."

It was quite ironic. The girl I had felt so connected to, so attracted to since the first moment I saw her, was like me. She was half-demon like me. Perhaps that was where our connection came from. That was why I felt so drawn to her, and wanted to protect her.

Like me, she was a sheep in a land of wolves.

"Nothing will happen to you," I promised her, because I

wouldn't let anything happen to her. "All you have to do is keep your magic hidden."

She snorted. "I didn't even know I had magic until a few moments ago. Who says I can control it now?"

I shook my head. "I don't know."

Her golden eyes became even brighter with unshed tears.

I took her hand in mine, trying to comfort her. I rubbed my thumb over the mark on her wrist. Was the mark staying because she had demon blood? Or the mark had somehow activated her demon side? Or the demon had marked her because he had sensed demon magic in her?

So many questions, and no clue where to search for answers.

I stroked my thumb over her wrist again.

This mark ...

Wait. Didn't Brianne, the girl who committed suicide, have a similar mark? I remembered the physician telling me about unusual tattoos.

Fuck.

I had to check on that. Right now.

I stood up, startling Erin. "What is it?"

"Hm, I need to go somewhere," I told her. I tugged her up. Holding her arms, I leaned closer and stared in her eyes. "Listen to me. Stay alert and keep your head down. Usually magic is connected to emotions, so try to stay calm. Say you're sick, if you have to, and stay in your room while I check on some things."

She frowned. "What things?"

"I'll tell you when I find out more." I ushered her to the front room of the library. "Remember, lay low," I warned her one last time.

She nodded once.

With that, I rushed out of the library. I didn't like leaving her alone like that, but my gut told me I was finally on the right lead and I needed to check it now.

I ran to the side of the Iris building, checked to see if anyone was close by, and shapeshifted into a raven. By far, turning into a raven was the coolest trick I gained when I found out I was half-demon and embraced my destiny with Asmodeus. I didn't use it much, especially here at the academy, but today it was a necessity.

I flew to the third floor of the Aster building, where the school archives were. At this time of the day, the place was supposed to be empty and locked. Despite my ranking with the academy, I didn't have free access to this room yet. Professor Crimson had been the one to convince Randall that I could easily change my grades if I had the keys to the place.

As if I couldn't enter the room any other way.

I reached the ledge of the window, knowing the lady who worked here always kept one of them cracked open because it got too musty inside, she said.

I flew into the archive room and shifted into my human form again. As expected, the room was dark. I conjured dark-fire in my palm, one like the one Erin had cast, and glanced around. Until a decade ago, all the files were on paper—there were rows and rows of shelves with boxes filled with students' and professors' files. It would take forever to transfer it all digitally.

Thankfully, I didn't have to search through the shelves for the file I wanted. Since Brianne had been a first-year student, her file was electronic. I took the chair behind the front desk, fired up the computer, and searched for her file.

I read through the file and clicked on the tab about her

death's investigation. There were even photographs of her dead body in here.

Despite the bad feeling in my gut, I dreaded finding the truth, and when I did find it, I wasn't ready.

My stomach dropped when I saw a picture of the girl's wrist—she had the same mark as Erin.

15

I HAD GONE TO MY ROOM, LIKE REY HAD INSTRUCTED, AND HAD every intention of remaining there for the rest of the day. I would say I was sick, just like he had suggested. But then Claire showed up. She noticed I was nervous, assumed it was because of Ava and Harvey, and before I could protest that I was sick, which she clearly had seen I wasn't by now, she dragged me to our next class.

I should have gone with the original plan—told her I was sick and went back to my bedroom—but at the same time, being alone right now scared me. Until a couple of hours ago, I hadn't known I could do magic. I had never done magic, not even by accident. All I had to do was forget about the last two hours. Pretend they had never existed.

Which was easier said than done.

I had been so out of it, I forgot what my next class was.

Magic spells.

With Professor Martha.

Shit, I was doomed.

I paused in the doorway. Claire frowned at me. "What is it?"

"I—"

Professor Martha appeared behind us. "You have three seconds to get in the classroom before I give you an absence."

Claire and I scurried inside the classroom and took our places, while the professor strolled in and dropped her things on her desk. She immediately launched into her lecture, as she usually did. In magic spells, we learned how to identify different types of spells and how to combat them. Today, the topic was dark magic from witches.

It was an interesting subject, but instead of paying attention to her, my mind wandered.

I had cast a spell. I had summoned, what was it? Darkfire, Rey had called it. I was half-demon, he said. Was he right? Or was I half-witch? Not that it was better, but who knew? Right now, all I knew was that there was magic inside me, and I had no idea how to control it.

What if I used it again, this time without meaning to? I should have stayed in my bedroom.

Shit, shit, shit, this couldn't be happening to me.

Fear and dread swirled inside me. I looked down at my hands, afraid of myself. The feeling was so intense, I leaned forward on my desk. If I had been standing, I would have crumbled to the floor.

Suddenly, students screamed. I snapped my head up and saw them getting up from their desks and crowding into the middle of the classroom. The room darkened and a heavy scent of rotting flesh filled my nostrils.

"Oh my goodness," Claire yelled, grabbing my arm.

I felt it. Before I saw them, I felt them. Vampires and werewolves and demons stood in the corners of the room—but they didn't look right. They seemed like zombified versions of the real thing with gray, decaying skin, missing hair, and gapping teeth.

I felt them because I had created them.

Stop, I ordered myself. *Stop!*

But nothing happened.

My fear and despair grew. The zombies advanced. Chaos ensued.

The students tried attacking the zombies as if they were real demons.

Claire held on to me, her hands shaking with fear. I tried disentangling myself from her before I ended up hurting her again, but her grip on me was suffocating. My panic threatened to overcome me, and with it, the zombies of the supernaturals turned stronger.

I closed my eyes, wishing, praying, chanting it would go away. That I could somehow regain control and make them go away.

A zapping sound echoed through the room. When I looked up, Professor Martha danced around the room, with her Dawnblade in her hand. She cut through the zombies, causing them to explode in a cloud of dust.

In a couple of minutes, all the zombies were gone, but the students didn't relax.

"It's okay now," Professor Martha said. "Those were illusions created by powerful magic. A demonstration of what you may encounter out there."

"That was terrifying!" Ava snapped. Several students muttered their agreements.

"I'm sorry it was too much," Professor Martha said. "I'll make sure not to repeat it."

"I thought it was cool," Harvey said, a cocky grin on his lips.

"Me too," Peter said. "That would be cool for sparring."

"Right!" Harvey agreed.

"Since this seemed like an intense experience," Professor Martha went on, ignoring the boys, "I'll dismiss class early today. You may go now."

Still shocked, but relieved at having the class cut short, the students grabbed their stuff and headed outside.

My insides were still tight, and my hands still shook when I picked up my books and headed to the door.

"Erin," Professor Martha called. Claire and I halted and looked at her. "Come have a word with me."

Claire shot me a glance, but she scurried out of the classroom like a scared mouse.

Holy shit, what could the professor want with me?

I swallowed hard and approached her desk. "Yes."

Professor Martha lifted a finger, telling me to wait. She watched as the last student left the room and the door closed behind her. Then, she turned her eyes to me. "You need to learn to keep your magic under control."

My jaw hit the floor, but I quickly picked it up. "I d-don't—"

"I know it was you," she said calmly.

Fear clogged my throat. "You're going to turn me in," I rasped, feeling a little dizzy.

Professor Martha shook her head. "No, I won't. I owe a great debt to your aunt, and to honor it, I won't turn you in. But you can't expose yourself again. You need to be careful." She frowned. "I've got something to help you with that. Come with me."

A little wary, I followed Professor Martha to her office in

the Aster building. There, she opened a drawer behind her desk and picked up a thin, silver bracelet.

I stared as she made her way to me. "What's that?"

"This bracelet will contain your powers," she said, reaching for my arm. She clasped the bracelet around my wrist. "Just don't take it off."

I frowned at the bracelet. "Are you sure this will work?"

She nodded. "I am."

"Thank you," I muttered.

"Don't thank me yet," she said, returning to behind her desk. "Your punishment for sneaking out might have ended, but because of your magic, we'll continue meeting at four in the morning for training."

I gaped at her. "What? Why?"

"Because you need to be the best demon hunter out there if you want to remain in this academy. You also need to be the best at hiding your powers when your emotions get the best of you. We'll continue training so you're in control of everything."

I hated the idea of waking up so early again, but if she could teach me to hide my powers, how to fight while keeping them hidden, then I was all for it. "Okay."

"Now go." She waved me off. "Remember to be careful."

I nodded. "I will."

With my mind buzzing, I walked out of her office and closed the door. Holy shit, I had conjured zombie-like creatures and Professor Martha had caught on and found out about me. If she had done that in such a short time, I was certain the other professors would too.

I was doomed.

As I made my way to my dorm room, a new thought sneaked into my mind. What if Professor Martha was lying?

What if she had a plan to expose me? How long did I have until she told my secret to everyone?

Once more, I found myself lost in this place, where I was supposed to belong. Which was so ironic now. If I was half-demon, I certainly didn't belong here.

Was there any place I belonged?

16

AFTER COPYING BRIANNE'S FILE FROM THE COMPUTER IN THE archive and printing it, I read it dozens of times. By now, I knew it by heart, but I still read it, as if new information would suddenly pop up.

Brianne had been an orphan, who moved to the school last year. She started as a second year, like Erin was, and then she committed suicide. Besides that and a short report on the facts about her death, there was no other information on her.

This girl might as well have been a fucking ghost.

I had been so focused on my research, I hadn't gone back to find Erin. Although, later that night, I had heard about the commotion in her magic spells class. I was sure she had been the one to summon the creatures and scare everyone. I bet she had scared herself too.

I wanted to go to her then, but it had been late. I had been sure she was sleeping.

The next morning, I timed it so I would find her after her training with Professor Martha, before her first class in the morning, but apparently, my timing was off. I hadn't found her in the cafeteria, or at her dorm. I waited for her to come out of her room, but she never did.

Was she hiding? Or had she gone directly from her training session to her class?

She wouldn't have run away again, would she? If she had, I would have heard about her missing by now ... wouldn't I?

An urge to skip my class and go after her rushed through me, but if I wanted to gain even more of Randall's trust to find out his weaknesses, I needed to have perfect attendance and perfect grades.

So, I dragged my feet to demon history.

Half my mind was in class, the other was on the situation surrounding Erin. That damn mark ... why did Brianne have the same exact mark on her wrist? Had she been kissed by the same demon? When? How?

So many questions swirled in my mind; I was going fucking insane.

Suddenly, a girl started crying in class. The professor stopped talking and everyone turned to her. She kept crying, clueless that she was interrupting the class.

"Harper?" the professor called her. She didn't hear him, or she couldn't answer. He called her again. When she didn't answer, he walked to her and touched her arm. She jumped, startled. "What's the matter?"

She only shook her head and cried harder.

The professor glanced at me. "Rey, would you mind escorting Harper to the infirmary?"

Yes, I minded, but I wouldn't say that to a professor. I stood up. "Of course."

The girl was so out of it, she barely noticed as I tugged on her elbow and guided her out of the classroom. It was only when we exited the building into the sunny day that she blinked and stared at me with misty eyes.

"I'm sorry," Harper said, crying even more.

"For what?"

"For having to deal with me," she whispered. "I'm a mess."

I stayed quiet. I really didn't have time to worry about other peoples' lives. If she needed help, all she had to do was ask for it. I didn't go poking around people's business.

I tugged her forward, and we continued to the Daffodil building.

She sniffed. "It has been hard, you know?" I rolled my eyes. Didn't this girl have any friends? "It's just … I miss Brianne."

I almost tripped over my feet. "Brianne was your friend?" She nodded. "You must know I investigated her death. I asked to talk to her friends, but no one came forward."

"Sorry about that," she said. "I just couldn't bring myself to talk to you or the other guards. If I did, then it would make it all so real." A sob cut through her throat. "I was in denial."

"I understand." I thought this over. She was upset. If I started firing questions at her, she would cry more and not answer anything. I had to be smart here. "I'm sorry for your loss."

She nodded. "First, we lost Cindy, and now Brianne." She let out another sob.

I frowned. "Wait, who's Cindy?"

"She was supposed to be in the second year with Brianne," Harper said. "The three of us were really close, even though I'm a year ahead of them."

"What happened to Cindy?" I asked, my voice low, respectful.

"She was murdered during the summer."

I inhaled a long breath. "I'm so sorry." This was too much of a coincidence.

"I'm ..." She shook her head and pressed her lips tight.

"You what?" I urged, curious. "Tell me."

We stopped in front of the Daffodil building. Harper turned her red-rimmed eyes to me. "I've lost my two best friends. I'm afraid I'll be the next one."

My eyes immediately lowered to her arm. She didn't have the demon mark on her wrists. What did it mean?

"That won't happen," I said, and for some reason, it felt like I was lying. "Come on." I escorted her inside the infirmary, where I told Cecile to give her something to calm down.

Then, I repeated my action from yesterday. I went to a corner of the building, where no prying eyes could see me, shifted into a raven, and flew to the archive room in the Aster building. Problem was, Sandra, the lady who worked there, was seated in front of the computer.

Thinking quickly, I summoned my powers and created a distraction—an eerie voice and shadow calling her from outside the room.

Sandra shot up, startled. Slowly, she approached the door and spied out. In raven form, I edged inside the room through the crack in the window. Once she stepped out to check on the bodiless voice, I shifted back into my human form, and closed the door behind her, locking it from the inside.

"What the—?" She jiggled the knob from the outside, but without the key, she wouldn't be able to come in. I heard as she stomped away, probably to get a spare key, or call someone to break through the door for her.

Which meant I had a few minutes to check Cindy's file.

Thankfully, there had been only two Cindys in recent years, but one had already graduated, and the other was dead.

I found it easily. Like Brianne, Cindy Tommen had also lost her parents when she was young. She had been raised by godparents. She had been brutally murdered during the summer, outside of the academy grounds, and from the report included in her files, she had been brutally killed by a demon, but no one knew which one.

I copied Cindy's file, shapeshifted into my raven, and flew out the window. I went directly to my dorm. I shifted back into a human, fished the keys from my pockets, unlocked my door, and entered my room.

I fired up my laptop, printed out Cindy's file, fished Brianne's file from my drawer, and put Cindy's beside it. I compared the two, but besides being orphans and being at the academy, there wasn't any other connection between the two.

Unless ... I logged into some social media websites. I searched for Cindy Tommen and found several pictures of her and her godparents that she had posted during the summer. In most of them, I could see she had the same fucking mark on her wrist that Brianne and Erin had.

What the fuck did that mean? That whoever had the mark was killed by a demon? Then what? Erin was next?

I took three long steps toward the door, intent on finding Erin, and being by her side until I found out what was going on, and how to stop this demon before he killed her too, but when I opened the door, one of Randall's secretaries stood in the hallway, her hand raised to knock on the door.

"Oh, glad to find you here," she said. "Randall is asking for you."

"I see," I said, trying to think of an excuse. "You can sa—"

"He said to drag you there if I had to." She tilted her head. "I won't have to do that, right?"

I wanted to see her try. But I got the fucking message. The headmaster wasn't happy and I was supposed to be there ten minutes ago.

I exhaled through my nose. "I'm on my way."

17

ERIN

IT SEEMED THE BRACELET PROFESSOR MARTHA GAVE ME WAS working well. Since I had started using it yesterday, I hadn't caused any accidents, and I couldn't even feel anything awake inside me—not that I was trying to. If I had my way, I would pretend there was no magic in my veins until the day I died.

When I got to martial arts class, I found a note on the door. Apparently, Professor Genevieve wasn't feeling well, and we were supposed to go to monster identification instead.

Along with the other students, I dragged my feet to the Orchid building where monster identification was held. I bumped into Claire on the way.

"I'm guessing your class changed too?" I asked.

"Yeah," she said. "I was supposed to have demonic spells, but because Professor Genevieve is sick, they moved around classes. I think this is the first time this has happened."

In the usual classroom, Claire and I took our seats. I felt Harvey's flirting stares and Ava's hateful glares bouncing off my head, but I didn't even look their way. Yesterday, I had been intent on playing with Harvey and irritating Ava, but things had changed. The fewer interactions I had with anyone at the academy for now, the better.

Professor Eleanor marched into the classroom. "Put down your books and pens. We're having a test." Protests and groans rose from the students. I admit I groaned too. A few feet from me, Harvey cursed his mother. If she heard him, she pretended she didn't.

"Why put down the pens?" Stella, one of Ava's friends, asked.

"Because it'll be a practical test," Professor Eleanor said. "The grades of this quiz will determine your partner, with whom you'll work with for the rest of the semester. Now, come forward and make a single line here."

For a couple of minutes, the classroom was filled with the sound of desks being dragged back, the shuffling of feet, and whispers. Once all our desks were squeezed in the back and we were in a line, the professor opened the door and let four guards enter.

"What are they doing here?" Harvey asked. If I was not mistaken, that was the first time he had spoken in this class without being spoken to first.

"They will help with the test," his mother said. "Here's how the test will work. The guards will attack you, and a picture will pop up on the projector." She pointed to the white wall behind her. "You have to be able to defend your-self and tell me the name of the supernatural in the picture and any important characteristics they have. If it's a demon, I need to know its ranking too."

Claire nodded.

"Are you agreeing to this crazy idea?" I asked her in a low voice.

"It'll be intense, and I'll probably fail the defend yourself part, but I see her point," Claire said. "She wants to see how we would react in a real situation. Fighting enemies and making judgments in high-stress situations."

High stress situations ... would I lose control of my magic again? I touched the bracelet on my wrist. In a few minutes, I would know if the bracelet really worked.

The test began and moved quickly. Peter was first. He fought off the guards' attacks and described the witches on the projector, even their coven name and what kind of magic they possessed.

Next was Harvey. Despite the tough act, he did well, which made his mother proud.

A few students went on. Some passed, some failed.

Then came Ava. She walked among the guards with an easy gait, full of confidence. I was sure this would be a breeze for her. I was shocked to see as she hesitated when the picture of a demon showed up on the projector. She stammered half names and forgot about the guards. Soon, she was on the floor.

Ava failed.

She cursed hell and heaven as she stomped to the back of the room.

It was Claire's turn. Like she predicted, she knew all about the fae on the projector, but she didn't even try defending herself. The guards took her down in three seconds.

She also failed.

"Erin," Professor Eleanor called.

Swallowing hard, I stepped forward, among the four poised guards. Shit, this was really happening.

I positioned myself like Professor Martha had taught me —feet apart, knees bent, core hard, hands up.

"Begin," the professor said.

The guards came at me.

I took a step back, avoiding two of them, then ducked from the other two. I landed a side kick on the shoulder of one guard, making him stumble over a second one, then spun back to escape from a roundhouse kick, and landed a back kick on the chest of another guard.

The picture of a beautiful woman with long silver hair, brilliant blue eyes, and pointed ears showed up on the wall.

"Frost fae," I said. One of the guards came at me. "They have ice and frost powers." I blocked a kick that would have hit me in the chest. When the guard punched at me, I deflected his strike, grabbed his wrist, twisted it, and landed a nice roundhouse kick to his chest. He stumbled back. "It's said the frost fae were banished from their realm, and now live on Earth, hiding up north."

Another guard lunged at me.

"That's enough," Professor Eleanor said. "Pass." I stared at her, a little shocked with myself, but she was scribbling something in her notebook atop her desk and wasn't paying attention to me. "Next!"

I forced my feet to move as the next student took my place.

Claire patted my shoulder. "I knew you could do it."

"Well, that makes one of us," I said.

Harvey winked at me. "Well done."

I fought the urge to roll my eyes at him. "Thanks."

A few feet from us, Ava grunted.

The rest of the students had their turns and their grades decided. Then, the professor started pairing up people according to their grades.

"Peter and Stella," she read from her notes. "Claire and Ava."

"Oh no," Claire muttered at the same time Ava shouted, "What?"

Professor Eleanor lifted her eyes from her notes and glanced at Ava with indifference. "If you wanted a better partner, you should have done better." She went on, "Harvey and Erin."

I stared at Harvey, and he smiled at me.

Ava clenched her fists and clamped her lips. I could see the three hundred curses she wanted to fire at me, at the professor, for the pairings, but she held it in.

Well, if I could, I would like to switch too. I would rather work with Claire than with Harvey. Poor Claire would have to put up with Ava's shitty attitude.

"For the semester's final project," the professor started as we sat down at our desks, beside our new partners, "you'll work on a project about a kind of demon. I'll go around the room now, telling you which demon your group will be assigned."

Instantly, Harvey put his elbow on his desk, propped his head on his hand, and stared at me. "I'm liking this project already."

This time, I did roll my eyes.

A moment later, his mother stopped by our desks. "You two got Garrimps." Then, she walked off to the next group.

Harvey didn't move. He kept staring at me.

I flipped through my book, trying to find the demon she had assigned to us. To my surprise, it was the freaking imps that had attacked me that night at the haunted house. If Rey had told me their names, I had long forgotten.

Rey ...

I turned to Harvey—the freak was still looking at me with puppy eyes. "So ... yesterday, I noticed you don't like Rey."

Instantly, Harvey lost his grin. He sat up in his chair. "Was that noticeable?" There was a hint of sarcasm in his voice.

"What is that all about?"

"There isn't much to tell," he said. Why did I get the feeling he was lying? "Just ... he's not a good guy. In fact, I would say he's downright evil. He might be fooling the headmaster with his tough act, but he doesn't fool me."

"What do you mean?" I probably had never been this curious in my entire life.

Harvey shook his head. "If I were you, I would stay from him."

I wanted to press him for more, but I knew he wouldn't tell me anything. With that, his flirting halted for the day, and the mood while we worked on our project soured.

I tried forgetting about Rey, but how could I when I was trying to learn about the little imps he had saved me from? If he was evil, wouldn't he have let me die? But then, what did I really know about him?

Nothing. The truth was, I knew nothing about Rey.

And I kind of hated that.

18

WHEN I ENTERED THE HEADMASTER'S OFFICE, RANDALL WAS standing in front of the tall window behind his desk, overlooking the campus's front gates. Looking at him like this, standing like a normal human, like a normal hunter, only in much fancier clothes, it was hard to believe he was a powerful immortal.

What would happen if I handed the killing blow right now? If I threw my Dawnblade at his back, right where his heart was? Would he die if it pierced him? Or would he sense it and deflect the blow before the blade even got close?

It would be too risky to try it now. If I failed, I wouldn't get another shot at it.

I closed the door and halted a good ways from his desk. "You called?"

Slowly, Randall turned around. "I did." He stared at me, his dark eyes intense. Hard. "How's the investigation going on Brianne Charles's death?"

I frowned. The investigation had been closed long ago. "It was ruled a suicide."

"I know you don't believe that," he said, his voice calm. Way too calm. "And I don't believe that either."

I opened my mouth to tell him about Cindy and the strange mark, but thought better of it. I didn't trust Randall. Until I knew more, and until I made sure Erin was safe, I couldn't tell him anything.

I shook my head. "I've been investigating it, but I've found nothing unusual," I lied. "So far, everything ties to suicide."

He narrowed his dark eyes at me. "I put you in charge of the security because you're the best student this school has seen in decades, and yet, you're doing a poor job keeping it secure."

"I'm trying—"

He slapped the desk. Leaning forward, he said through gritted teeth, "Don't lie to me, Rey."

"Sir, I—"

"I know of your deal with Asmodeus," he told me.

My blood chilled. "I don't know what you heard—"

"Don't lie to me, Rey," he repeated, interrupting me again. "I know Asmodeus is your father and he tricked you into an impossible contract. And now he has asked you to kill me."

"How ...?" I asked in a whisper.

"I can help you out of your contract with Asmodeus," Randall said instead, surprising me even more. Why would he do that? "All you have to do for me is kill your father."

Didn't he think I knew that if I managed to kill my father, my contract would be void? But Asmodeus was even more powerful than Randall. I barely had any fucking chance of killing Randall. Killing Asmodeus? Never in any of my dreams.

"If it was that easy, I would have already done it," I told Randall.

"But you didn't have my incentive, did you? Kill Asmodeus, break your contract, and I'll let you become a real demon hunter."

The frown in my brows deepened. I didn't doubt he could do it, but I was curious about exactly how he would do that. Demon hunters were born. I was able to use a powerful witch's spell to trick them all—except for Randall. I should have known he wouldn't be fooled. If he could see through the spell, perhaps he could make me into a real demon hunter.

That was ridiculous.

I shook my head, pushing those thoughts out of my mind. "I have one question though. If you knew all that, if you knew I wasn't a real demon hunter, I was a half-demon and Asmodeus's son, why did you let me join the academy? Why did you let me stay? And why did you favor me above all other students?"

"You think I'd reveal all my secrets to you? All you need to know is that I have my reasons." He sat back in his leather chair. "I'll give you some time to think about my proposition." He waved me off. "I'll call for you when I need your answer."

I hesitated. Mostly because I was still too fucking shocked to process everything I had heard, not because I wanted to talk more about it. Holy fuck, as if I didn't have enough on my plate, now I had to worry about Randall being on my back too?

Things were never boring around here.

I started back to my dorm room. I hadn't made it halfway there, when the warning bells rang in my mind.

I cursed under my breath.

First Randall, now Asmodeus was calling me.

I went to the side of the Aster building, checked if I was

alone, and shapeshifted into my raven. I flew over the academy walls, over the forest at the base of the mountain, and into Liberty Creek. Even though the town was five hours by car from the academy, I could fly much faster than that. In an alley, I shifted back into my human form. I looked down at myself. Fuck, I still had the school uniform on. I took off the jacket with the academy crest and the tie, folded them over my arm, and walked out of the alley.

As usual, Asmodeus was waiting for me in the corner booth of the pub. He had his whiskey in his hand. The waitress brought a second one for me the moment I sat down across the table.

"There is my favorite demon," he said, his tone amused. Was he drunk? I doubted it. "How's the academy?"

I frowned. "Why did you call?"

"Well, because it has been over two fucking months and you haven't killed Randall yet." His amused expression was gone, replaced by a glare. "What the fuck have you been doing there that you didn't have time to kill him?"

My jaw worked hard. "You gave me until the end of the semester. I still have time left."

"I gave you that much time because I was being considerate," he said. As if he had ever been considerate in his long life. "I never thought you would actually take this fucking long to end him."

"It'll be more difficult now because Randall is aware of our deal," I told him. "He knows you want me to kill him."

Asmodeus shrugged. "I don't care if he knows. I want it done." He leaned forward on the table. "Get it done, Rey, and get it done soon, or I'll use my will against you. You know that if I call you to the underworld to stay beside me, you won't be able to say no."

The fucking contract. When Asmodeus ordered me to do something, I couldn't disobey him.

"I'll do it," I said, though I didn't feel as confident as my words. "Just give me until the end of the semester, as you first promised."

Asmodeus watched for a moment. What I wouldn't give to understand his mind. If I could understand how his mind worked, then I could defeat him.

Finally, he took a long swallow of his drink and said, "Fine. You have until the agreed time to kill him." He pointed his index finger at me. "But you better not fail me, Rey. You don't want to know the consequences if you do."

I nodded once, drank my whiskey in one gulp, then stood and walked out of the pub. It was still early in the day and I had classes to attend, but the day was rather nice with the warm sun and almost no clouds in the sky. I shoved my hands into my pockets and walked around, trying to keep my mind blank.

Who was I fucking kidding? My mind was never blank.

Instead, I agonized about everything. First, there was Erin and the fucking demon mark. I still had to investigate that more. I needed to find out which demon was after her, and if he was really going to come for Erin.

And now this dilemma that would get me killed or sent me to the underworld as punishment. Randall versus Asmodeus. Who would be easier to kill?

None. Neither of them would be easy to kill. And even if I could, I was sure it would be suicide. I would only kill them, after using all my power, and probably dying at their hands.

Why couldn't there be a fucking easy answer for once?

19

ERIN

"I HEARD WE'LL HAVE *ONLY* SPARRING TODAY," CLAIRE SAID AS we made our way to the Hyacinth building. Her martial arts class was later, but she insisted on walking with me before heading to her class.

I had already sparred with Professor Martha at four this morning. What was a little more sparring? Truth be told, Professor Martha had kicked my butt, and every muscle in my body was sore. At least, she made a mumbled comment that I was improving. Slowly, but improving.

I glanced at the sky. It was a warm fall day. The trees around the campus were full of orange and red, which I always thought was pretty. Except for the Blackthorn tree, which was always black and had no leaves, only many thorns.

Despite my best efforts, my mind stirred to the first time when I saw the Blackthorn tree—when Rey brought me here.

Rey. I hadn't seen him in almost two days. He said he would confirm something then get back to me. I guessed he either hadn't confirmed anything, or he was running from me. I mean, I couldn't blame him. I was half-demon after all.

Claire waved goodbye in front of the Hyacinth building, and I joined the other students around the mat and started stretching.

Across the room, Ava looked like a gymnast. She touched her entire chest to her legs while grabbing her feet. Then, she pulled one leg to her head, or bent sideways, over one leg.

Freaking show off.

Well, if I were as flexible as she was, maybe I would show off too.

In matter of minutes, Professor Genevieve entered the classroom. "Arrange in a wide circle and sit down," she said simply, not offering any explanation about being sick two days ago and canceling our class.

Mutters spread through the students while we positioned ourselves at the edge of the mat in the center of the room. It seemed everyone was apprehensive about sparring.

"Peter, Harvey," the professor called. "You're up." The two young men jumped up and met in the center of the ring. The professor raised her hand, then dropped it. "Begin."

Harvey and Peter charged each other. Both were tall and strong, which made for an even match. They blocked and dodged and parried most of the attacks, and the match went nowhere. Finally, after five minutes, the professor called it.

"Stella, Harper," the professor said. "You're next." Harper paled before she stood and met Stella in the center of the ring. "Begin," the professor said.

Stella came for Harper. Until now, everyone had been going easy on her since she was still unwell after losing her best friend, Brianne. But Stella didn't seem to care. Of course, she was friends with Ava, wasn't she? A bitch for a bitch.

Harper barely had time to defend herself before Stella brought her to the floor.

Professor Genevieve marched into the ring and interrupted the fight. "What is this?" She turned her hard stare on Harper. "You call that a fight? That was ridiculous."

"I-I'm sorry," Harper stammered. Her shoulders folded forward. I could see she wanted to curl up or disappear.

"I don't want an apology; I want a fight." The professor pointed to the door. "As punishment, go run five laps on the indoor track. After class, we'll have a talk."

Harper lowered her head and dragged her feet to the door. I felt myself rising, to go after her, to talk to her and try to make her feel better—even though I had never said more than five words to her before—but stopped after I saw Ava and her friends chuckling from the other side of the room. No, right now, I didn't want to go after Harper. I wanted to kick Ava's ass.

The professor made my dream come true. "Ava, Erin, your turn," she said.

I sprang to my feet and let the fury I felt for Ava fuel me. I was thankful the bracelet was secure on my wrist, or I was sure I wouldn't be able to control my magic. Shit, I wanted to wipe Ava's smug smile from her face.

She halted in front of me, her hip to one side, one of her hands on her waist. "Ready to be beaten to a pulp?"

"I want to see you try," I said through gritted teeth.

"Begin!" the professor said.

Expecting her move, I took a large step to the side when she lunged for me. I spun around and brought my fist across, landing a block on her chest. Gasping in surprise, Ava took two steps back.

"What the—?"

I advanced on her. She lifted her arms up, but I twisted

for a side kick and pushed through to her waist. Once more, Ava stared at me as if she had never seen me before.

"That's it!" she cried as she opened her arms and swiped wide for me, like a wild animal. I ducked under her arms and retreated.

Hm, I was sure I hadn't seen that move in this class, or my training with Professor Martha, but since the professor hadn't called me on it, I let it go.

This time, Ava advanced. I blocked her roundhouse kick, but she didn't drop her leg and landed a second one on my shoulder. When she dropped the leg, it was right in between mine, and she punched my lower belly.

I stumbled back, out of breath.

What the freaking hell!

I inhaled deeply, trying to ignore the pain. Before I had half a second to recover, she was at me again. With her long legs, Ava reached me with a turning side kick, but I hopped back and out of range. Then, she spun and went for a back kick. It hit me in the ribs.

"Holy mother of—" I bit down on my words as the pain spread through my chest.

She offered me a cocky smile.

Bitch.

For the next two minutes, we went back and forth. Ava landed a roundhouse kick to my chest. I punched her gut. She blocked one of my kicks and kicked me instead. I placed a beautiful side kick to her back—she almost fell forward and kissed the floor. One of her punches grazed my chin—it would leave a damn mark—and I kicked her in the side.

The professor's clap echoed through the classroom. "You can stop now," she said. Reluctantly, Ava and I retreated, both of us limping. "That was a great, well-matched fight. It was nice seeing you two taking advantage of your space, spinning out of range, and attacking from behind. It was so good, I didn't want to stop the watch, but at seven minutes, I had to, otherwise the others won't have time to spar." She faced me. "I can see you've been training outside of class. I like your dedication. Keep it up." Then, she gestured to the door. "Now you two go to the infirmary to check if any of your injuries are serious."

Ava and I limped to the door. She tried to push me out of the way, but I took a large step away from her before she could. What? She wanted to keep going even if we were not in class anymore? Well, for her bitchiness, I would, all she had to do was look at me the wrong way.

But, as I went down the front stairs of the building, moaning as my sore muscles screamed and pain ricocheted through my body, I realized the adrenaline was almost gone. I wouldn't be able to fight again, not right now.

Not caring about Ava, I dragged my feet to the infirmary as fast as I could. Cecile greeted me in the foyer. "Oh, don't tell me Professor Genevieve had another sparring match?"

"She did," I said with a groan.

"This is the third this week." She walked to me and held my arm. "Yesterday was both the third and first years, and I had six students come to me." She tsked. "I think this afternoon she'll do the same with the fourth year."

Fourth year. I bet Rey could kick everyone's ass.

I shook my head. "Well, if it makes you feel any better, that's my adversary." I pointed my chin to the door. Ava limped inside the infirmary.

Cecile chuckled. "You gave as good as you got. Good girl. Now let's get you checked."

* * *

I WAS THANKFUL FOR TWO THINGS: I WAS PUT ON A STRETCHER far away from Ava, and was able to keep the curtain around my bed pulled closed so I wouldn't see her face across the room. And I had no broken bones or extensive damage.

Cecile recommended some rest and to apply ice to the bruise on my shoulder, and some ointment to the graze on my chin.

"I've contacted the professors of your next classes," Cecile said. "They know you'll be taking the rest of the day off to rest. But please, rest. Go to your dorm and sleep if you can. Tomorrow, you can return to your normal activities, just no sparring or intense exercises for at least two days."

Professor Martha wouldn't be too happy about that.

"Thanks," I told her.

She nodded and walked away.

Then Rey, his face whiter than usual, his gray eyes huge, appeared in front of me. "What is it? What happened?"

"I'm fine."

"You don't look fine." His gaze skimmed over me, searching the wounds. "Were you attacked by a demon? Where? Which demon?"

"Rey," I called. Though I was enjoying seeing him worried —about me or the academy security?—I didn't want to prolong his suffering. "It wasn't a demon."

He frowned. "Then what happened?"

"Martial arts class. I sparred with Ava."

"Oh." His shoulders relaxed, but his eyes narrowed at the purpling wound on my shoulder. "Did you take something for the pain?"

I nodded. "Cecile gave me something." I put my legs

down and Rey reached for my arm. "I'm fine. I won't fall. I promise."

He took two large steps back. I hopped out of bed. "How did you know I was here?"

"I was between classes when I heard you were in the infirmary." He ran a hand through his dirty-blond hair. "I didn't think; I just came here."

I fought against the smile threatening to appear. He had been gone for two days, but once he heard I was hurt, he came running. My heart skipped a beat, then hammered against my ribs.

"Well, as you can see, I'm okay." I walked around him.

He turned and caught up with me. "Where are you going now?"

"To my dorm, to rest."

"Right," he said.

He followed me out, always close. I felt that if I tripped, he would catch me half a second later.

Outside, I halted and faced him. "That day, at the library, you said you would go check on something, then you would get back to me about it. I'm guessing you're not done checking whatever it was."

"About that ..." He let out a long sigh, then looked around. Some students headed to other buildings. "How about I take you to your dorm and we talk there?"

I frowned. Rey in my dorm room. It somehow felt wildly inappropriate, but at the same time, somewhat intimate. I liked the idea of him there.

I nodded.

Together, we went to my dorm. At the stairs, I reached for the handrail, but Rey caught my hand and hooked it on his arm. He helped me climb the stairs, then opened the door of my room for me.

Inside, with the door closed, I felt self-conscious. Suddenly feeling warm, I sat on the bed. Rey took the chair in front of my desk.

"So ..." I urged him.

"Right." He ran his hand through his hair again. "Remember Brianne Charles?"

"The girl who committed suicide?"

"She had the same mark on her wrist." He pointed to me.

I turned my wrist. The damn mark was still there, no signs of fading. "You mean this one?"

He nodded. "And one of her best friends also had it."

"Had it? As in the past ..."

"She was murdered by a demon last summer."

My hand flew to my mouth. "So ... you think we are connected. That the same demon who marked me marked them, and now they are ..." I sucked in a sharp inhale. "This means I'm the next one."

Rey shot to his feet. "I won't let anything happen to you." He had said the same thing before. The will and power of his tone hadn't changed.

I appreciated his enthusiasm, but I didn't feel so assured. He had been gone for two days. What if this demon came when he was far from me again?

"You haven't figured out what kind of demon he is?"

He sat down beside me. "No, not yet."

I frowned. "Wait, didn't you kill the demon that night?"

"I did, but I'm starting to think that the demon was one of many, or he was a minion of a bigger demon."

Shit. I glanced at the mark on my wrist. An idea sparked in my mind. "We could try summoning him."

"What?"

"I mean, is that a thing? Summoning a demon?"

"Yes, but—"

"Then we should do it," I said, feeling oddly sure about this idea.

"You want to summon the demon who wants to kill you? That doesn't make sense."

"I can either wait for this demon like a sitting duck, or I can get ready, summon him, and kill him." I paused. "But I need your help. I doubt I can kill it by myself."

Rey shook his head. "I don't like this idea."

"It's not that I like it, but do you have any better ideas?"

He stared at me with those intense gray eyes. "Are you sure about this?"

I started nodding but then shook my head. "I just think it's better than to be sleeping and have the demon slit my throat in the middle of the night."

He flinched. "Fuck," he muttered under this breath. "When you put it that way, I guess it's better to face him with a plan."

My stomach twisted in a mix of anticipation and dread. "So ...?"

Rey let out a long breath. "All right. We'll summon it this weekend."

I frowned. "Why this weekend?"

He gestured to me. "So you can recover."

"Cecile's medicine is working," I told him. "I barely feel any pain, just some soreness." But soreness was part of my life now. "We should do it soon."

His thick brows slammed down. "When do you want to do it?"

"We summon the demon tonight."

20

I DIDN'T LIKE THIS IDEA. I REALLY DIDN'T LIKE THIS FUCKING idea, but like Erin said, it was either summoning the demon, or waiting until he came for her.

It was close to midnight when we sneaked out of the dorm. I had told Erin to dress in all black and bring her aunt's sword. She still didn't have her own Dawnblade, but if things got ugly and I couldn't deal with the demon alone, I would need her help. It was better if she had a sword in her hand than trying to punch a demon in the face, especially if he was a powerful one.

Erin approached me, showed me the sword, and whispered, "I'm ready."

The moonlight bathed her fair face, and for a moment, all I could do was stare at her. She had a fitted thermal tee, leggings, and boots—all black, like I had told her. Her long black hair was pulled up into a ponytail, showing off more of her pretty face. And her eyes ... her golden eyes seemed to shine even more in the dark.

She was so fucking beautiful, it hurt.

I cleared my throat. "Then let's go."

We crept up past the dorms, around the Daffodil building, to the side of the Iris building. Ava and Claire walked out of the library. When they saw us, they halted.

Ava put a hand on her waist and opened her mouth to speak.

But I was faster. "What are you two doing here at this time?" I asked, using my professor-like voice. I had heard there was a verbal bet going with the fourth-year students. After I graduated at the end of the school year, I would become a full-fledged hunter, or since Randall favored me, I would become a professor.

Neither, I wanted to tell them. I wouldn't become either.

"We were working on our monster identification project," Claire said, not sounding too pleased.

Erin frowned. "It's almost midnight!"

"If we want to present a good project, we have to work hard, don't we?" Ava flipped her blond hair like the little bitch she was. Just because almost everyone in her family had become a legendary demon hunter, she felt entitled.

Claire leaned closer to Erin and whispered, but not too low, "Since she failed the last test, she wants to do well on this project to impress Harvey's mother again."

"Hey!" Ava protested. "That's not it."

Claire shrugged.

"Regardless of the reason, you two should return to your dorm now," I said, still using my authoritarian tone.

Ava tilted her head at us. "What about you two? Or at least Erin? Curfew was hours ago."

Claire's eyes went wide. "Erin, what's going on?"

I glanced at Erin. We had to send them away.

"It's nothing," Erin said, with a small, fake smile. "You two should go."

"Why should I go when you won't?" Ava asked.

"I'm staying with you until you go back too." Claire grabbed Erin's arm. That was when she noticed the sword in Erin's hand. She took a step back. "Why ... why are you carrying a Dawnblade?" Claire frowned. "I didn't even know you had one."

"It's not mine," Erin said. "See?" She shook the sword. "I can't summon it and make it disappear like you guys. This one is my aunt's."

"You two are up to something." Ava crossed her arms. "I want to know what it is."

I groaned. "We don't have time for this." If we wanted to make it across the wall, we had to go now.

"Please, just go back to your rooms," Erin pleaded.

"You're scaring me." Claire took Erin's arm again. "If you want me to go back to my room, you have to come with me."

"Me too," Ava said.

"I don't think they will leave," Erin said to me.

"Then we give up," I muttered.

"No." Erin shook her hand once. "We have to do this tonight." She glanced at Claire and Ava. "We'll let you tag along, but you have to be quiet and do what we tell you to, okay?" Claire nodded. Ava didn't. "Ava, I'm talking to you too."

She rolled her eyes. "Fine."

"I don't like this," I said.

Erin jerked her chin forward. "Let's just go."

The bad idea turned worse. If it had been only Claire, I wouldn't have minded as much. Claire was quiet and she seemed to like Erin a lot, which made her a good friend. But

Ava? I could see her running off while we were summoning the demon to call the guards or Randall.

If she did that, I would—

No, that was the demon in me talking. I wouldn't hurt her, but fuck, I would want to.

Deciding to focus on the next part of our plan, I trudged forward, but halted at the corner of the Hyacinth building. I had changed the schedule of the guards tonight, just by a few minutes, to give us access to the back gate.

The girls stopped behind me and waited.

I glanced at my wristwatch. Just one more minute.

The two guards at the outpost walked away for their patrol. The other two guards should be a few yards away, but because of the change I made, they wouldn't be in range.

"Now," I told them.

I ran to the outpost, the three girls on my heels. I fished the keys from my pocket, unlocked the gates, and ushered them through it. Then, I stepped out, locked the gate again, and ran into the forest with them.

When we were hidden by the trees, I stopped and glanced back. Three minutes later, one of the guards appeared at the gate. He looked around, but not seeing anything, he entered the outpost.

"Holy crap, that was scary," Claire said.

Erin smiled at her. "A little, but also exciting."

So, the thrill of forbidden things excited her? I wasn't sure it was a good idea for me to know that.

"Let's keep moving." I took the lead again and guided them deeper into the forest, away from the running trails. Because of my demon blood, I could see well in the dark, but I had brought a flashlight in case Erin still couldn't. I turned it on and illuminated the way.

"So, are you two going to tell me what's going on?" Ava asked.

"I don't think so," I barked, already irritated with her.

"I want to know too," Claire said.

"Well …" Erin started. "A few months ago, I was marked by a demon." She rolled up the sleeve of her thermal tee and showed them the mark. "Rey found out Brianne and Cindy had this same mark, and now they are both dead."

Claire gasped. "You mean, Brianne who committed suicide?"

"We don't think it was suicide," I said.

"What? You think it was a demon?" Claire asked, sounding more shocked by the second. "The demon who gave you this mark?"

"Yes," Erin answered.

"I remember Cindy," Ava said, her tone somber. "She was friends with Brianne."

"And Harper," Claire said.

"Right," Erin said. "Though Harper doesn't have the mark. As for Brianne and Cindy, we don't know any connection between their cases other than this mark, but since I have it, we don't want to take any chances."

"What do you mean?" Ava asked.

"We're going to summon the demon," I said simply.

Claire halted and Ava tripped.

"You're going to do what now?" Ava almost shrieked. "That's … that's crazy."

"It's dangerous," Claire whispered.

"If we're caught summoning a demon, we'll all be expelled from the academy," Ava protested.

I turned to her. "You're the one who insisted on coming. If you don't want to witness this, then go back the way you came. You won't be able to go through the gates until we do, so you are welcome to sit tight and wait. Otherwise, shut the fuck up and do what you're told."

I marched forward, Erin by my side. I heard Ava and Claire's footsteps catching up with us, but I didn't acknowledge them. If I had my way, they wouldn't have come. At least, Erin hadn't told Ava about being half-demon. I was sure that secret wouldn't last long if she knew.

Finally, we arrived in a large enough clearing.

I immediately started marking the summoning circle. With my Dawnblade, I cut my palm, shallow so it would heal nicely, but long enough that blood seeped from it. Holding out a fist, I let the blood drip to the ground, forming a crude circle. Inside the circle, I drew the mark on Erin's wrist.

"Erin." I held out my other hand to her.

Expression strict, she stepped into the circle and stood beside me. I took her hand in mine. "I'm sorry."

She nodded. "It's okay."

I aligned the tip of the Dawnblade with her fingertip and pressed it. A fat drop of blood appeared. I turned her hand down and the drop fell in the center of the mark.

"Let's back away." Still holding her hand, I retreated until we were out of the circle. Ava and Claire stood beside us, the two of them tense and worried.

A moment later, I felt it. The power surging in the summoning circle—through it. A dark glow shone through the circle lines.

"Oh my gosh," Ava whispered.

The glow intensified until we couldn't stare at it anymore. I brought an arm over my face, and Erin turned her head to the side, toward me. Then, the glow was gone.

The demon stood in the middle of the circle.

"Fuck," I muttered.

Verin, a general of Prince Paimon of the underworld, turned his eerie white eyes to us. I had seen him before, in his human form, but right now, he seemed like the king of the underworld. Long, powerful limbs made of sinew and black muscles and gray bones. Long fingers like claws, razor-like teeth, and two black horns curled on top of his head.

He radiated power and death and hunger.

Hunger for Erin.

Verin zeroed in on Erin. "You dare summon me," he said, his eerie voice echoing through the clearing. His forked tongue sneaked out of his mouth and ran over his nonexistence lips. "Your scent." He inhaled deeply. "I'll savor devouring you."

Pale like a ghost, Erin's hand closed around my wrist.

My Dawnblade poised by my side, I stepped in front of Erin. "Not if I kill you first." I entered the circle.

Verin swiped his hand wide. I ducked underneath it and slashed his side. Which made me pause. What the fuck? This demon was supposed to be powerful. It should be hard to get to him.

Unless ...

Verin let out a hoarse laugh as he turned to me, his side intact. Dark shadows gathered around him. "That didn't even tickle." He threw his hand out, and his invisible power hit me square in the chest.

I flew several feet and landed hard on my back, gasping for air.

"Rey!" Erin shouted.

The demon turned to her. "You're mine." He advanced toward her, but was stopped by the circle. He punched the invisible wall containing him, and the air around us fluttered. The damn circle wouldn't hold him for long.

Gritting my teeth because of the pain, I pushed to my feet.

On the other side of the circle, Erin stood in front of the demon, her hands shaking around her Dawnblade. "Go back to hell!" she screamed as she swiped the sword, aiming for his wide chest.

Verin laughed as he slapped the sword away before it even got close to him. The Dawnblade fell to the ground, and Erin stumbled with the force of the impact.

Partially breaking through the circle's protection, Verin reached his arm forward and grabbed Erin's shoulder.

"No!" I yelled, running to them.

Erin screamed as the demon dragged her inside the circle. I lunged at his back, my sword raised. His power hit me like a cannon, pushing me away from him.

This time, though, I was able to land on my feet, and immediately ran back to them.

"Do something!" I screamed at Claire and Ava. "Help us!"

Ava looked around, searching for something she could use.

"Your Dawnblade, dummy!" Claire yelled.

With a half-smile, Ava extended her hand and her sword appeared. She ran into the circle.

"Let me go!" Erin screamed, fighting against the demon's grip around her shoulders.

He opened his mouth wide, ready to feed on Erin.

Then, I landed on his back, and Ava came at him from the side. We both slashed through him, probably only tickling him, but it was enough to distract him enough for him to lose his grip on Erin.

Erin scurried back and I cut his back again. "Look over here, you little shit."

"Little?" His voice boomed through the air. "You dare call me little." Trying to scare us, the demon grew. First, he was a head taller than me. Then, he grew ... three heads taller. Five heads taller. Then, he was easily two of me, maybe even three. At this size, the circle couldn't contain him.

"Did you have to say that?" Ava yelled.

"I came for the girl." Verin's voice carried through the forest. "But I'll devour all of you now."

He leaned down and reached for Ava. The girl screamed and ran.

He might have grown bigger and stronger, but it also made him a little slower.

"Claire," I shouted. "His name is Verin. He's a general under Paimon of the underworld. How do we defeat him?"

She closed her eyes and thought for a moment. Meanwhile, the demon still chased Ava, who hadn't stopped screaming.

Erin raced to me. "Are you okay?"

I touched her, my hand on her waist. It felt good knowing she was safe. "I am, but if we don't find a way to kill him soon, he'll win."

"I know!" Claire shouted. She ran to us. "We have to—"

The demon turned to us. I grabbed Erin's hand and pulled her to the side, but not before running my Dawnblade across his leg. Claire raced to his other side. Following my lead, Ava slashed the demon's other leg.

Once more, our strikes barely tickled him.

"Come to me," Verin said, his big hand going for Erin.

"Get to Claire," she said, freeing her arm from my grip.

"Find out what to do." Then, she ran in the opposite direction.

She was distracting the demon, while we came up with a plan.

My chest constricted with an emotion I wasn't ready to name.

I sprang into action. I found Claire and went to her. "What do we have to do?"

"To be honest, I'm not completely sure, because he's a higher-ranked demon, it could not work at all," Claire started.

"Just tell me," I urged her.

Ava joined us. "I'm here."

"All right." She pointed to the circle. "We have to stand on the perimeter of the circle and pierce the Dawnblades into the ground. That will create a powerful cloud around the demon, and he will be frozen for a few moments. I know we only have two swords here, but it should work, even if only for a moment."

"And then?" I asked.

"Then ... Erin needs to pierce his chest, right in the middle," Claire said.

"Erin?" I inhaled sharply. "Because she's the one with the mark."

Claire nodded. "Right."

"Hurry up!" Erin screamed from a few yards away. She skidded in the dirt, just as his hand dipped down for her. Then, she veered off. Her chest heaved; she was getting tired.

"All right, let's do it." I looked at Ava. "You stand directly across from me." She nodded. I turned to Claire. "Summon yours." Claire didn't seem happy about it, but she didn't argue.

With our swords in hand, we took our positions on the circle's perimeter. "Bring him into the circle," I told Erin.

Breathing hard, she ran back to us. Once she stepped into the circle, she asked, "What now?"

"When the demon comes in, stand there." Claire pointed to a spot in the circle, directly across from her. "Use your aunt's Dawnblade and do what we do."

Erin picked up the sword and waited. With a roar, the demon lunged at her, both his hand swiping for her. Erin ducked under his grasp and took her place in the circle.

"Now!" I cried.

I pierced the Dawnblade into the ground, directly over the blood line marking the circle. Erin, Ava, and Claire did the same.

"What—?" Verin looked around. Then, he let out another roar. Dark shadows swirled around him.

The shield's power created by the swords slammed against his chest, the force of the impact shaking the earth and the Dawnblades. I gritted my teeth and held it as steady as I could.

His blast gone, the power of the shield spread, creating an invisible cloud around the demon. The intense power drove him to his knees and paralyzed him.

"You only have about a minute!" Claire shouted.

I left my Dawnblade buried in the ground. "Erin, come with me."

Together, we stopped in front of the demon. Verin's muscles trembled as he tried to move. A gurgled roar came out of his mouth.

"What do I do?" she asked. Her hands shook around her sword, her eyes were wide, but she was determined.

My chest tightened again.

I shook my head. I stood behind her and reached over, closing my hand over hers. "We'll kill it now, okay?"

She nodded.

With my strength, I pulled back her arm and pierced the Dawnblade through the demon's chest.

This time, his roar sounded loud and clear. I pushed the sword a little bit, to make sure it struck home, then pulled it out.

The invisible cloud faded and the demon swiped at us. Erin and I jumped out of the way.

What? It hadn't worked.

But then, the demon let out a shuddering breath. His body folded forward and black blood seeped around him. The earth beneath us shook again, but this time, it didn't stop.

"What is that?" Ava asked.

We all retreated to the edge of the clearing and watched as the earth within the summoning circle crumbled and turned inside out, making the circle and the blood disappear, and taking the demon with it.

* * *

"What the hell was that?" Erin asked once the earth had stopped shaking and was back to normal.

"The demon's name is Verin," I told her. "He's a general under Prince Paimon from the underworld." I paused, unsure if I should go on, but also unwilling to hide this from her. "Paimon is King Brikan's most loyal prince."

"King Brikan?" she asked, her face pale. "You mean the king of the underworld, the supreme demon?"

I nodded. "That's the one."

"Wait, you're saying Prince Paimon was the one who marked Erin?" Ava asked, her face full of disgust. "What for?" She glanced at Erin. "What's so special about you?"

Erin lowered her gaze.

"This is crazy," Claire whispered. She attached herself to Erin again. "I'm worried about you."

Me too.

To be honest, I was freaking out right now, but I didn't want to scare them, scare Erin, anymore. Not right now, at least.

"I think we've done all we could for one night," I said, trying to regain some control over the situation. Because even though we had gotten rid of the general, there was still the prince of the underworld for us to deal with. We had solved nothing. In fact, we probably made everything worse by killing such a powerful demon.

"Yeah," Erin said, her voice detached. "We should go back and get some rest."

In silence, we reached the back gate. We waited for the next hole I had created in the watch schedule, then we sneaked inside the academy. I escorted the girls to their dorm.

Then, I turned to Ava and Claire. "What happened tonight ... you two can't tell anyone."

"You think I want to tell anyone about this?" Ava asked. "First, they will think I'm crazy. Second, they'd expel me. No, thank you. I'm taking this to my grave."

"You better," I warned.

She humphed, then marched inside the building.

Claire lagged behind with Erin. Didn't Claire have a clue?

Did I have to spell it out that I wanted her gone so I could talk to Erin alone?

But it was Erin who spoke first. "Thank you for helping me tonight, Rey."

I frowned. "I'm not sure we did anything good."

She offered me a small smile. "But we tried."

"Erin ..." I started, but Claire's presence was like a thorn from the Blackthorn tree. "Hm, just, be careful. Always stay within the school walls, and please, don't be alone, except for when you're inside your room. If you need to go somewhere, please take Claire, or even Ava, if you have to."

Claire nodded. "I won't leave her alone even for a minute."

Erin frowned and asked in a low voice, "What happens now?"

I sighed. "I don't know, but I'm going to try and figure it out. For now, just be careful."

"I will," she whispered.

I watched as the two of them entered the building. I didn't move until the light in Erin's room came on and then turned off again a few minutes later as she went to sleep.

Then, I headed to my dorm, where I would probably not sleep at all, while I obsessed about what the fuck we had done.

21

ERIN

AFTER TAKING A WARM SHOWER AND SOME PAIN MEDICATION for the increasing soreness in my body, I lay in my bed, but despite how worn out I felt, I couldn't sleep. I closed my eyes and tried to rest, but my mind was filled with eerie images that were sure to give me a nightmare—Verin appearing before us; the way he looked at me as if he planned to eat me and licked his fingers afterward; the demon chasing me and his claws almost grazing my skin; and me plunging the sword into his chest.

That noise of wetness and something being squished, that resistance from his muscles and bones, that scent of rotting and death.

I would never forget it.

Besides that time when the little imps had attacked me and I had used the Dawnblade, this was the first time I had stabbed someone. I knew he was a demon, he was evil, and it was best if he was dead ... but I had done it. I had pierced his chest and killed him.

I would forever be grateful for Rey, who held my hand

and guided me through it. If he hadn't been there, I would have chickened out and not done it. Right now, I would be dead, eaten by that same demon.

It was a little funny, actually, how Rey knew that. He knew I wouldn't be able to do it, that I probably wouldn't even have the strength to do it, since I had never wielded a sword.

Afterward, my stomach turned and I thought I would throw up at my feet. Thankfully, I was able to keep the contents of my dinner inside my belly.

I still felt queasy just thinking about it, though.

An hour after I lay down, I got up. It was time to train with Professor Martha. I was so freaking excited.

Not.

I dressed in my training uniform and met her in the Hyacinth building. We started with stretches and then simple hand and foot techniques. But I couldn't focus. There was no power behind my punches and my blocks, and no height to my kicks.

"Wait," Professor Martha said as I was about to start another series of combinations. I stopped and looked at her. "What's wrong with you?" She did nothing to hide her annoyance. "You look like a zombie going through the movements."

"I didn't sleep much last night." It was a lie; I just didn't need to elaborate on it.

"Are you worried about something?"

I shrugged. "Just school stuff," I lied. But perhaps ... perhaps I could lie some more and get some information from her. "Professor Eleanor said we'll have another pop quiz soon and it'll be about higher-ranked demons." I paused. "I was wondering if you could share anything you know about the princes of the underworld."

Professor Martha's body went rigid. "Why would you want to know about the princes?"

"Well, aren't they just under the king of the underworld? Besides him, they rule the underworld. We're studying demons and how to kill them. Shouldn't we know more about the ones who command them all?" I braced myself, hoping my half-assed answer was good enough.

"You'll learn about him in your third year," Professor Martha said. "If Professor Eleanor is teaching you about him now, then I need to have a talk with her."

"No," I said quickly. "She mentioned the higher-ranked demons and some princes," I tried amending my lie. I was sure to be caught. "I'm the one curious about them."

Professor Martha looked at me for a moment. I thought she wouldn't answer, or yell at me to keep training without talking, but then she let out a long breath and said, "Think of the underworld as a kingdom. Brikan is the king, and the princes are the second in command. They were created by the king eons ago, and each of them have legions of demons under their control. They are very powerful, almost as powerful as the king. Most can shapeshift into any animal and some can even shapeshift into humans." She paused. "And while I'm on that subject, let me tell you about King Brikan. He is a horrible demon with powers unlike any other demon known to hunters. His magic is beyond imagining. He's often called the Supreme Demon because of it."

"He was born that way?" I asked, curious. Besides last night, this was the first time I was hearing of him.

"Brikan is the last remaining original demon who was formed after the creation of Earth, millions of years ago. No one knows his exact origin. All we know is that several millennia ago, he rose to power by slaying the rest of the original demons and taking control of the underworld. Those who don't serve him, fear him."

I frowned. "Are there any known ways to kill him?"

She shook her head. "It's rumored he's impossible to kill."

"If he's so powerful and impossible to kill, why doesn't he attack the academy and kill all the demon hunters?" I asked. "I'm sure it would make his life easier if no demon hunters existed."

"Our headmaster is legendary," Professor Martha said. "He's also too old to count and extremely powerful. I bet that if the two of them ever faced off, the rest of the world would be destroyed before the two could hurt each other." She pressed her lips together, then continued, "It's said that King Brikan doesn't want to kill us. He wants to enslave us, so we can hunt supernaturals for him. Only then he would be able to rise from the underworld and dominate mankind."

I stared at her. "This is ... wow."

"Yes, it is." Professor Martha nodded. "You must never talk about the princes and King Brikan to anyone, not until you're in the third and fourth year and Professor Eleanor teaches you more about it, understand?"

I nodded. "Yes, ma'am."

"All right," she said with a long breath. "Seeing as you're not at your best this morning, we'll end this session early. Go rest until your classes start later."

Before I could thank her for the thought, Professor Martha marched out of the classroom.

I stayed there for a few minutes, thinking about all she had told me. What could an all-powerful prince of the underworld want with someone like me? It didn't make sense.

But one thing I was sure of. If Prince Paimon came for me, my fighting skills alone wouldn't cut it. I was much better than a couple of months ago, but not good enough. I needed something more.

I looked down at my hands.

Determined, I walked out of the Hyacinth building and into the wooded area near the outer wall, where no one would see me—I hoped.

Holding my breath, I took off the bracelet Professor Martha had given me and placed it in my pocket. Then, I let out a long breath and focused.

Magic. If I were to fight a big demon, I would probably need my magic.

I closed my eyes and channeled my magic as Rey had taught me that day at the library. I felt the tingling sensation of my magic waking up inside me, the buzzing as it traveled through my veins, and filled my core.

Opening my eyes, I gasped in awe. Holy shit, I had magic. I didn't think I would ever get used to this.

I called the darkfire.

The black flame came to life in my open palm.

I smiled at it.

But it went downhill from there.

The darkfire grew and grew, becoming like a little tornado, spinning out of control. It grew bigger than my arm. I stepped back and it touched the ground, almost as tall as me.

My panic rose in my throat.

"Stop!" I ordered, trying to calm down my magic, to quiet it.

But it didn't work.

Then, the dark tornado moved in a circle, faster and wider with each turn.

I retreated more, but the damn thing kept coming, kept spinning, kept growing.

Then it hit me.

I fell on the ground as pain spread through me, like a thousand tiny spiders biting my skin and spreading their poison. I twisted on the ground, biting my lip to contain my scream. Holy shit, it burned.

I didn't know how long it passed, but finally, the pain lessened and I was able to sit up.

The darkfire was gone. It probably dissipated once it exploded.

I glanced at my hands. I was still sure my magic was the only thing that could save me—maybe—but I wasn't so sure about this method.

In a place full of demon hunters eager to kill their enemies, I was better keeping this quiet. If I couldn't learn magic, then I would have to find another way to defend myself.

But how?

22

REY

MY FIRST CLASS OF THE DAY WAS DEMON HISTORY. AS USUAL, Professor Graham gave us a long lecture about some chapter, then handed us a sheet of paper with several questions for us to answer. All easy work.

But this time, Professor Genevieve sneaked into the class-room. "If I may borrow Rey, please."

"Of course," Professor Graham said.

Whispers echoed around the room while I picked up my books and walked out the door.

"What is it?" I asked, following her down the hallway.

"This way," she said simply.

Outside the building, a small group of students had gath-ered. The professor clapped her hands twice, catching the attention of everyone. The other students and I formed a circle around her.

"What's going on?" Peter asked me in a whisper. I just shrugged.

"Now that you're all here, we can begin," the professor said. "Since you are the best demon hunter students in the academy, you were assigned a task today: patrol the campus and report on any demon sightings."

"Demon sighting?" one student muttered.

"Are there demons at the academy?" another one asked.

"It doesn't make sense," a third one commented.

"That's impossible!" a fourth one exclaimed.

"And what are we supposed to do if we find one?" Harvey asked, crossing his arms. Of course he would be here.

My curiosity over the task turned sour.

"If you can, kill it," Professor Genevieve said. "If you can't, contain it until help arrives."

"Professor ... demons?" Peter asked. "The academy is secure, is it not?" He glanced at me. "Is it not?"

The professor tsked. "It's an exercise. Pretend it's real." She looked down at a chart in her hand. "Now, I'll assign you all in groups of two. When I call your names, you can start walking the grounds, preferably close to the outer walls. Then meet me back here in an hour." She scribbled something down then said, "Rey and Harvey."

Holy fuck.

Reluctantly, I set off with Harvey. We walked close to the back wall and I took this opportunity to check on other details of security, and find some clues about what happened last night.

I still didn't understand why that demon had marked Erin. Was it really for Prince Paimon? Or was something else going on there?

If we found a demon lurking, I could interrogate him before killing him. Perhaps they would know something.

But as we walked—in tense, uncomfortable silence—we didn't find anything. Not a demon, not a clue, not even a fucking leaf out of place.

Finally, our hour was almost up, and we made our way back to meet Professor Genevieve.

"I told Erin to stay away from you."

Couldn't he have stayed fucking quiet for another five minutes? It would have been so much easier. And his comment really didn't help. "She can do whatever she wants." In fact, I often found myself hoping she would come to me any time of the day and night.

Harvey shook his head. "No, she can't. She shouldn't."

I halted. The blood in my veins started to boil. "Why is that?"

"Don't pretend you're a saint." He turned to me, his chest puffed. Harvey was almost two years younger than my human age, but he was just as tall as I was, and a little wider. Still, with my demon blood, he could never take me on. "In fact, you're evil."

I clenched my hands. "I don't care about your opinion of me."

"I know what you are, remember? You can't fool me."

Holy fuck.

I had met Harvey before he joined the academy. He was known in the demon hunter world because of his mother and father. Everyone expected great things from him. Even though I tried keeping to my own, Harvey and I hit it off. We became friends.

One day, when I was in my second year, Randall sent me on a solo mission. My guess was that he was testing me, seeing if he could trust me, before taking me under his wing. He sent me after one of the generals under Asmodeus's command. At that point, I didn't think he knew what I was, or who my father was, so I went on with the mission, determined to find a solution. I would either let the general escape, or talk to Asmodeus and have him agree that I could kill the general to gain Randall's trust as he wished.

But what I didn't expect was for Harvey to follow me. He showed up when I was battling the general, and even though he wasn't trained yet and didn't have his own Dawnblade, he wanted to help me.

That was when Asmodeus showed up. He got a kick out of the entire thing and instead of fighting me, or Harvey, he went after Harvey's parents and uncle, who were on patrol in the mountains. Asmodeus almost killed them. Harvey's father recovered, but his mother was severely hurt, and his uncle died.

To make things worse, Asmodeus revealed I was his son to Harvey. Then, my father disappeared, leaving us to clean up the mess he had created.

After that, Harvey never forgave me. He felt betrayed, and I couldn't argue he was wrong. For some reason, he stayed quiet about my secret, but he kept his distance from me ever since.

"You know why I never told anyone about you?" he asked, surprising me. "Because the headmaster ordered me not to. He said that if I told anyone, I would be expelled from the academy, my mother would be fired from her teaching position, and my father would be dismissed from the Blackthorn hunters."

"Fuck, Harvey, I didn't kn—"

"But," he started, interrupting me, "if you don't stay away from Erin, I will tell her. Hell, I'll tell everyone." He leaned closer and bared his teeth at me. "You're a bad guy, Rey. Realize that, and do Erin a favor. Stay. Away. From. Her."

He marched toward the meeting point in front of the class building. I stayed frozen in place for a moment.

Fuck, he was right.

When I was around Erin, something in me changed. I became someone else. I pretended my world wasn't upside down, and there was a good solution to everything. A happy ending. When, in fact, there wasn't. As a half-demon with a contract with a prince of the underworld, who happened to be my father, there wasn't a happy ending. There never would be.

But ... I couldn't just let her go right now. There was too much danger around her. If I didn't keep my eye on her, if I didn't stay close and protect her, she could die.

I couldn't let Erin die. I just couldn't.

I couldn't stay away from her.

Perhaps there was something else I could do. I could come clean and tell her about me. After all, she was also a half-demon. If someone in this entire place could understand, it was her.

But could I simply open my mouth and tell her all the fucked up things about myself? That was the real question.

23

ERIN

THE MORE I TRIED TO FIT IN, THE MORE OF AN OUTSIDER I FELT. I came to the academy late and had to catch up on everything —rules, classes, training … I was doing better with those, but since finding out I had magic and was probably half-demon, I wondered if I was really meant to be a demon hunter.

What was my other option? Be an evil demon?

Nope. Not happening.

Two days passed while I gathered the courage to approach Claire and ask her for help. I tried putting myself in her shoes, if she came to me and revealed what she was, what would I do? Would I be afraid of her? Would I tell a professor? Would I listen? It was hard to say.

Finally, we were alone in the media room on a Saturday afternoon, lazing on the recliner couch and watching an old vampire movie, when I decided it was time.

I sat up suddenly and said, "I'm a half-demon."

Claire stared at me with huge eyes. "What did you say?"

"A few days ago, Rey and I found out I have magic," I said. "Demon magic. Rey thinks I'm a half-demon."

She sat up beside me. "You're not joking."

"No, I'm not." I shook my head, then let out a sigh. "It feels so good to finally tell you this. I've been walking on eggshells for days now. But ..."

"But?"

"I'm worried you'll hate me," I confessed. "I'm afraid you'll be afraid of me and turn me in to the headmaster."

Her brows curled down. "I'm a little shocked, but I don't hate you and I'm not afraid of you. Although, I'm worried you'll get caught. Who else knows about this?"

"Just Rey, you, and me." I thought for a moment. "Oh, and Professor Martha."

"Oh, she knows too?"

"Yeah, she caught me. Remember the zombies in her class? It was me."

She gasped. "Really?"

"Yup. After finding out about my magic, I panicked. Professor Martha noticed it was me and she gave me this bracelet." I showed her the thin silver chain on my wrist, the same one with the demon mark still etched on my skin. "It contains my magic."

"That's unexpected," she whispered. "I would have thought she would have arrested you, or worse."

"Me too." I frowned. "You aren't afraid of me? Really?"

A small smile spread over her lips. "Was this your choice? I bet it wasn't. You were born this way and it's not your fault. You're the one who just found out about this and is probably scared out of your mind."

"I am," I told her.

She patted my hand. "Everything will be okay."

"It won't unless I can learn how to control my magic." I told her about trying to replicate the darkfire and only end up hurting myself. I needed a teacher or at least some kind of tutoring. Maybe if I searched online, I would find tutorial videos? If only.

Her eyes sparked and she stood up. "I know."

I stood beside her. "What do you know?"

"My father has a library with books about all kinds of magic at home," she said. "I bet some have detailed spells you can try."

That sounded great, but ... "How are you going to get the books?"

Claire winked. "Leave that to me." She started retreating. "Meet me in the Hyacinth building in fifteen minutes!"

With that, she dashed away.

What the ...?

Shaking my head, I went to my room and changed into the thermal tees and tactical pants we wore for martial arts class—in case I needed to move quickly with the spells— then headed to the Hyacinth building.

Afraid someone would see me and ask me what was going on, I waited for Claire inside. The building was eerily quiet and dark. I almost regretted being cooped up inside, where my imagination took off. At least I was wearing the bracelet, and my emotions wouldn't dictate my magic right now.

Claire arrived at the building not fifteen minutes later, but almost thirty minutes.

"I was about to go after you," I told her.

She gestured to the black backpack on her back. "It wasn't easy sneaking out with these."

"So you got them?"

"A few of them," she said, walking down the hallway. "He

has way too many. If these don't help, I can swap them for others."

"Let's hope we can figure it out with the first book we crack open," I wished.

Claire and I entered a small classroom at the end of the hallway, with windows covered by dark curtains, and only one door. This way, it would be harder for anyone walking by to see what we were up to. We left out pads and other martial arts accessories, just in case.

We cracked open the first book.

And we closed it.

"This shit is in some other language," I complained.

She opened the book again. "Crap, I bet this is a demonic language. We won't learn these until our fourth year."

I glanced at her. "You're telling me that you, the student of the century, don't know how to read this?"

Her cheeks reddened. "Well, I know several words, but I can't read sentences yet." She skimmed through the first page reading some of the words out loud.

"Okay, okay, I got it. Moving on." I opened the next book. This one was written in English. It detailed several spells used by witches.

"Did you know that the covens keep the heart of the first witch?"

I stared at her in horror. "What? Why?"

"It's what gives them power, or increases it at least. The first witch of their coven was supposedly the most powerful. So, after she dies, the other witches keep the heart, which is still beating, by the way."

I wrinkled my nose. "That is so gross."

"I know." She flipped a couple of pages, then pointed to a spell. "Here. Try this one."

I read the chapter, talking about conjuring a bolt of fire and molding it to your will. "I've tried this one with Rey, and I couldn't do the fire thing, only darkfire."

"Darkfire is demon fire," she said in a low voice. "Only demons can conjure it."

I gestured to myself. "Half-demon here."

"Right." She pointed to the page again. "Try it anyway. Even if all you can conjure is darkfire, then use that."

Inhaling deeply, I slipped off the bracelet and gave it to Claire. "All right."

I spread my legs apart and lifted my hand, my palm turned up. After another deep breath, I closed my eyes and focused on the magic inside me. I called it, willing it to fill my veins, to do my bidding.

Suddenly, an avalanche overtook me and I gasped for air. My magic overflowed my veins, my senses.

"Take control," Claire said, her voice loud. "You can do it."

I imagined a black river invading a house. I shaped the walls the way I wanted them to be, the way I wanted the river to go. I funneled the passage, so not all of it could pass at once.

Then, I imagined a bright red fire floating over my palm.

I opened my eyes. Once more, the flame was dark, not red. "Darkfire," I muttered, disappointed. I closed my hand, extinguishing the fire before I lost control over it again.

"It's okay. At least, you were able to conjure it and put it out," Claire said. She turned to the book again. "Let's try this one now."

From there, we tried several spells from the book. After a few, we noticed one thing: I could not perform any of the ones labeled "light" spells, only the ones labeled "dark" spells. Most of the time, when I tried a light spell, it turned dark, like with the darkfire.

"If I had my doubts before, I guess this proves it," I said, leaning against the wall. We had been at this for over an hour. It was pointless. "I'm really a half-demon." My stomach turned. Shit, that still sounded so foreign to me.

Claire faced me. "It doesn't matter, as long as you're good in here." She pointed to her chest.

How could she be taking this so well? I wanted to believe I would have had the same trust in her, but I seriously doubted it. She had a purer heart than I did. I would have been afraid, and probably avoided her.

Guilt and disgust made themselves known within me.

I slid down the wall and sat on the ground. "I guess I'll be using that freaking bracelet forever."

"Don't give up just yet," Claire urged. She knelt in front of me, a book in her lap. "We just started. I can see if my father has other books, with dark spells. Since that's your affinity, maybe if you practice those first, you'll get a better hang of it overall, and will then be able to perform light spells."

I frowned. Light versus dark. Why was that so important? All I wanted was to get my magic under control, be it dark, or light, or bright pink.

"My mood is gone," I grumbled. "Maybe we should stop for today and do something fun instead."

"Can I just tell you one more thing before you give up?"

"Go ahead."

Claire bit her lower lip before saying, "Why don't you ask Rey for help? He seems to know a lot about these things."

"About what things?"

She shrugged. "Like when we summoned that demon in the forest. He knew the exact name of the demon, his ranking, and which prince he worked under. I bet he knows a lot more about the underworld than these books. You're the one who said he helped you conjure your first spell."

What did I have to lose? Rey already knew about my magic and my half-demon blood. Asking him to help me wouldn't hurt.

Besides, it would give me an excuse to go see him on a Saturday.

I put the bracelet back around my wrist. "All right. I'll go find him."

She smiled at me. "Have fun."

Chuckling, I stood from the ground and walked out of the classroom.

I halted outside, though. Where could Rey be on a late Saturday afternoon? Patrolling the outer walls? Checking the outposts? Having meetings with the headmaster?

Out on a date with his girlfriend?

I shuddered.

No. If he had a girlfriend, I would have known, right? He would have told me. Or I would have seen them together around campus.

Right?

A little uncertainty snaked its way into my system, but I pushed it aside and set out for the place I thought I should cross off my list, in case I had to hunt him down: his dorm room.

Because of his status, I had first thought Rey lived in a townhouse on the other side of campus, in the Dahlia Villa with the professors and other staff. But no, he lived like any other student, in a dorm room in the Snapdragon building, which housed the male rooms.

I paused at the entrance of the building. Shit, I knew

there were times when females weren't supposed to enter the male dormitories, and vice versa, like after some time at night, and a bigger window on weekends, but I had never paid attention to that, because why would I enter the Snapdragon building?

Whatever. If I was caught, I would pull out the I'm-new-here card and hope I wasn't punished.

Holding my breath, I walked into the building. Three seconds later, Harvey exited the cafeteria and rushed to me.

"Erin, what are you doing here?" He flashed me a big grin. "Did you come to see me? Want to catch that movie I mentioned the other day?"

I glanced at him. Though he had kept his flirtation up, Harvey hadn't pushed me to watch movies or do anything else with him again. I wondered if he had made up with Ava, but seeing as he was all over me now, I hoped not—for her sake.

"Actually, I'm looking for Rey."

His smile faded. "You shouldn't hang out with him."

He had given me a similar warning before.

"Why is that?" I asked.

Harvey shook his head. "He's just not a nice guy, that's all."

I frowned. "That's not good enough." I headed toward the staircase.

His hand closed around my arm. "Erin, listen to me. Stay away from him."

I jerked my arm free. "Keep it up and I will stay away from you."

He raised both his hands in a sign of peace. "I'm sorry, I'm sorry. It's just ..." He pressed his lips tight and shook his head.

"You know what? Go ahead. Let him disappoint you and break your heart. Then, I'll be able to say I told you so."

Harvey took a large step back, clearly getting out of my way.

I stared at him for a moment. What the hell, dude? If this was his personality, then I really didn't want anything with him.

I climbed the stairs to the third floor, and followed the numbers on the wall, until I found his at the end of the hallway—I hadn't asked Claire how she knew his dorm number, because I really didn't want to know.

Loud rock music rang through the door.

I knocked on the thick wood.

Nothing.

I tried again, and got no answer.

It was impossible that he was sleeping with the music blasting through the walls, right? But he still didn't hear me knocking, probably because of the music.

"Rey?" I called, my voice loud, but not so loud that I would bother the other students. "Are you in there?" He probably was. Otherwise, there would be no music.

Shit.

Sure this wasn't the greatest idea I ever had, I twisted the knob and pushed on the door. I expected it to be locked, but instead it flew open.

Revealing Rey standing in the middle of the room, wearing only black pants—no shirt, no socks ...

And with a snake of darkfire dancing around him.

Fuck, fuck, fuck.

Erin wasn't supposed to see me like this.

I dropped the magic swirling around me and turned off the music. "Erin," I whispered her name, like a faint prayer that she wouldn't hate me.

Her golden eyes were huge and her face pale. "What—?" She pointed to me, her finger drawing a circle. "That ... it was magic. Darkfire." She narrowed her eyes at me. "Holy shit, you're a demon."

I raced around her and closed the door. Fuck, why hadn't I locked it? I had just come back from patrolling the entire campus and an intense meeting with Randall. I had been fuming, so I took a long shower to relax. But it hadn't worked, so I turned on the music, and let some of my energy burn by letting out my power. My head had been so out of it, I hadn't even noticed I hadn't locked the fucking door.

I never meant for Erin to find out about me like this. Despite dreading it, I had intentions of telling her everything about me.

"I can explain," I said. "Give me a few minutes, and I'll explain everything."

She hugged herself. "You have two minutes."

Two minutes wouldn't be enough to tell her everything, but I knew that as soon as I started, she would want to hear me to the end.

"Then, sit down." I gestured to the chair in front of my desk.

Erin sat down. Her golden eyes slid down to my chest. Her cheeks turned red and she looked out the window.

Fuck. I grabbed a black shirt from my closet and slipped it over my head. Underneath all the craziness of the moment, I was glad Erin had stared at me, and felt embarrassed about it. It meant she was affected by me—the same way I was affected by her.

I sat down on my bed, directly in front of Erin, and started. "I wanted to tell you this before, I just didn't know how or when. Because, yes, I'm a half-demon like you, but there's much more to my story than that." I inhaled deeply. "My real name is Reyan and I'm a thousand years old."

Her jaw fell open. "You, what?"

"My mother fell in love with a man and had my sister and me. That man abandoned us when I was a little kid. Years later, the man came to find me. He introduced himself as Asmodeus, one of the princes of the underworld. He said he wanted to take me with him, to become a prince. I refused. A year or so passed and the black plague hit the village I lived in. My mother and sister became sick. They were dying. I called for Asmodeus. I told him I would go with him if he healed my mother and my sister. So he did. Asmodeus healed them, but he also wiped their memories of me. They no longer remembered me. They didn't know who I was."

Sorrow lumped in my throat. "I remember feeling heartbroken. Lost. I hated Asmodeus for what he had done, but I couldn't change our contract. Not that I would have. Even if I knew the outcome, I would probably have still made the deal, because my mother and sister lived long lives and died of old age."

"You outlived them," she whispered.

I nodded. "Yes. Though they didn't know me, I kept close, always watching over them." Fuck, what was this painful emotion in my chest? "I watched them die."

"I'm so sorry," Erin said.

"Because of my contract with Asmodeus, I had to work for him. Whatever he tells me to do, I can't say no. It's futile to resist it." I fiddled with the speakers' remote control. "At first, I argued with him. The deaths were ... but after a while, it became normal. Dealing with demons, killing them, collecting contracts ... it was normal. It was like I was numb; my emotions were muted."

Until recently, when Erin showed up in my life. An urge to kneel in front of her, take her hands in mine, and tell her how much she meant to me hit me so hard, pain cut through my chest.

I couldn't do that to her, though. Even if Erin was a half-demon like me, she was so much better than me. I had done terrible things in my long life, and she deserved better.

"I can't imagine how horrible it must have been," she said, her golden eyes soft.

"I was sent here by Asmodeus," I told her.

She tilted her head. "You mean, you're not a demon hunter?"

I shook my head. "No. I'm half-human. Most of my demon hunter powers are actually from my demon blood. Asmodeus had a powerful witch cast a spell on me to trick the other demon hunters."

"What about the Dawnblade? I thought only demon hunters could wield it."

"True." I pulled mine from under the bed. I liked to keep it close when I slept. "Mine is a good replica, but not the real thing. I don't need its power to kill demons."

Erin stared at the sword. Was she afraid I was going to use it against her? I lowered it again, just to keep her at ease.

"Why did Asmodeus send you here?" she asked.

"To spy and send him information about the demon hunters," I told her. "When I first met you, I had just left a meeting with Asmodeus. He had asked me to come back to the academy for one last mission. If I succeed, I'll gain my freedom."

"What is your mission?"

"To kill Randall."

She gasped. "But ... that's impossible."

I nodded. "But Asmodeus is certain Randall has a weakness, and he wants me to find it. For that, I need to be close to Randall."

"That's why you are the head of the security."

"That's actually new," I said. "Randall handpicked me two years ago. He said he would shape me to be the best demon hunter ever. Professor Crimson soon started spreading rumors that Randall was training me to succeed him, in case something happened to him. But the thing is, Randall knows about me."

"You mean ..."

"Yeah, he knows I'm a half-demon, he knows who my father is, and he knows I'm here to kill him."

"And he still keeps you close."

"I think he finds it amusing." I frowned. "But he made me a proposition the other day. He wants me to kill Asmodeus and break my contract with him. Then, he'll let me live like a real demon hunter. No one will ever know that I'm a half-demon."

"Wow."

I chuckled, because that was exactly how I felt. Wow, this sucked. "Yeah. I'm caught between killing Randall or killing Asmodeus. No matter which one I choose, I'm most likely to end up dead too." I let out a long sigh. "But I do have to choose one. Because Asmodeus ordered me to kill Randall, I won't be able to resist for long, but if I kill Asmodeus in the meantime, then my contract will be broken." I shook my head. "Either way, it's an impossible choice."

Surprising me, Erin stood up, took three large steps, and sat down on the bed beside me.

"Whatever you choose, you'll end up free and be able to do whatever you want." She stared up at me, her face so close. "What is it that you want?"

Right now, I wanted to touch her. I wanted to close my hand around the nape of her neck, pull her to me, feel her warmth against me, and bring her lips to mine.

"I want to be free," I confessed in a whisper. I looked out the window, to the rays of sunlight streaming through the half-closed curtains. "But I don't deserve it. I have done some fucked up things for Asmodeus. I'm sure if I died today, I would go straight to the underworld, right back to his hands."

Erin reached over and placed her hand on my chest, right above my heart. "I'm sure you're being too harsh on yourself."

I stared at her hand for a moment, then lifted my eyes to hers. "No, I'm serious. All the fuck—"

"You did all of that because Asmodeus told you to.

He *ordered* you to. You had no choice." She tapped her fingers on my chest. "I'm sure that, right here, you're a very good person."

Those golden eyes ... holy fuck.

Every nerve and cell in my body screamed for me to take her. To lean over her, lay her down on my bed, press my body against her, and have her.

Holy fuck, how I wanted to.

But it wasn't right. It really wasn't right.

I stood up, putting some distance between the two of us. "Anyway, that's my story. Now you know everything about me."

She offered me a small, closed-lip smile. "Thank you for sharing all that with me."

"So, hm." I ran a hand through my hair. It was still damp from my recent shower. "Why did you come here?"

"Oh, right," she said, as if finally waking up from a dream. "I need your help. I've been trying to practice magic, so I don't lose control again, but I can't do it alone. Since you seemed to know a lot about it, I was going to ask you if you could point me in the right direction. But now I see you know more about magic than I first thought." She paused. "Would you mind teaching me?"

I should say yes, that I minded. Even though I had come clean and told her everything about me—minus the details of all the horrible things I had done—I was still the bad guy here. If she stayed near me, she would be in even more danger than she already was. But at the same time, how could I stand back and watch as the mark on her wrist attracted higher demons and the princes of the underworld and do nothing?

Until she was truly safe, I wanted to be by her side.

"Not at all." I poked my foot at my boots beside the door. "Let me put these on and we can go."

* * *

I took Erin to a secluded, wooded area near the north outer wall. The outpost at the northeast wall was farthest from here, and I knew the patrol schedules, so we would be ready when they approached.

I stood right in front of her. "Remember how you conjured darkfire?"

She nodded. "That wasn't the only time. I did it once more alone, and lost control. It became a huge tornado and hurt me in the process. The other time was earlier this afternoon, when I was trying to follow some spells Claire had found in her father's books."

Several thoughts filled my mind: One, Claire knew about Erin being a half-demon and having demonic magic, and she was helping Erin with it. Two, they had peeked at books they probably shouldn't have. If Professor Crimson found out about it, they were toast. Three, Erin had cast a tornado and hurt herself? She seemed okay now, at least.

"Good, then that means you should be able to conjure it again without too much work, right?" I asked.

"Right."

"Then let's start with that." I took three steps back. "Extend your hand and conjure a small darkfire."

Erin rolled her shoulders, then outstretched her hand in front of her. She closed her eyes for a moment. The darkfire came to life in her open palm.

"What do I do now?" she asked, her voice tight, as if she was straining with the magic.

"Now, we'll play with it." I lifted my hand up and conjured a small flame like hers. "Like this." I closed my hand and the flame went out. When I opened my hand, it came back. "Try it."

Her brows curled down as she focused. Erin closed her hand and the flame was gone. Good. But when she opened her hand again, the fire didn't come back instantly. It took a few seconds before it appeared in her palm again.

"Shit," she muttered, trying again. And again, the flame was delayed.

"It's okay." I dropped my darkfire and walked to her. "Don't try so hard. We're just playing now, okay?"

She glanced at me. "Okay."

Standing in front of her, I put my hand under hers. I felt her magic thrumming through her veins, unstable. I breathed in and out, willing it to ease up, to become steadier. "Close your hand again," I said. She did, and I followed her movement, my hand closing over hers. The flame was gone. "Open." She and I opened our hands, and the flame came back instantly.

She smiled at me—a big, proud smile that tugged at my chest. "I did it."

"You did." Ignoring the urge to hold on to her, I lowered my hand. "Now try it again."

Frowning, Erin went for it. The flame disappeared when she closed her hand into a fist, and it immediately showed up again once she opened her hand. "I really did it!"

A sense of pride overwhelmed me.

Holy fuck. If training with her would be like this, I was

screwed. How would I be able to contain my feelings, my fucking desire, when she smiled at me like that?

Channeling coldness into my heart—the same emotion I had been familiar with for so long, while I stole, tricked, and murdered for Asmodeus—I showed her other tricks, a little more advanced each time.

I showed her how to aim the darkfire and throw it at a target, and how to create a defensive wall in front of her. I also told her that darkfire was powerful and could hurt demon hunters easily, and lesser demons. What I didn't tell her was that, even if she got good at controlling and using her magic, it probably wouldn't be enough to protect her from a demon prince.

We trained for over an hour, until I could see Erin was getting tired and was losing control over the darkfire.

"That's enough for today," I told her.

Taking a deep breath, she glanced at the sky. I stared at her long neck, and the thin sheen of perspiration there.

I could lean over her, and lick her neck, bite her jaw, and—

I closed my eyes and shook my head.

Stay fucking focused, Reyan!

"It seems it's going to be a pretty night," she said, her eyes still in the sky.

I looked up too. The sky was darkening as the sun began its descent. There were no clouds in sight, which meant the moon would be bright and the dark would be clustered with stars.

I lowered my gaze back at her. "Are you hungry?"

She looked at me. "A little."

I should have sent her back to Claire, so they could have

dinner together, but right now, I felt selfish. I wanted to spend time with her, even if it was having dinner together in the cafeteria, surrounded by other students.

I beckoned her to come with me. "Let's go eat."

25

ERIN

WAKE UP AT FOUR IN THE MORNING TO TRAIN WITH PROFESSOR Martha, have classes all day long, study with Claire in the library in the evenings, go back to the gym to do weight lifting, then meet up with Rey late at night to practice magic—the next two weeks flew by.

Because of my intense schedule, my mood varied a lot. There were days when I felt my muscles stronger, my movements sharper and swifter. I felt good and energetic. But there were days when I slept poorly, my entire body felt sore, and I had to drag myself everywhere.

However, no matter how I felt, my late nights with Rey were always great. We met after curfew, when the students were supposed to stay inside the dorms. Thanks to the pass Professor Martha had given me, I had no trouble walking around campus late at night. Every time I got to the clearing, Rey was there, waiting for me with either a warm cup of coffee or hot chocolate.

My heart melted each time.

How could he be so handsome and caring? I knew he had

a dark past, but when he was standing beside me, his body angled toward mine, his face so close that I could smell the woodsy, spicy scent of his aftershave, his warm hand on mine, showing me what to do, his gray eyes shining almost silver, I forgot all about it. When my heart was beating so fast it hurt, and warmth coiled low in my belly, how could I remember anything? If he asked me, I probably wouldn't even remember my name.

That was how far gone I was.

And I had tried denying it. For days, I told myself I was being childish. It was just an attraction. I mean, he was so freaking hot, how could I not be attracted to him? That day I caught him doing magic in his room, he was wearing only pants, and I had taken a good look at his ripped chest. Each muscle hard as if it had been sculpted with a divine chisel —even that goddamn V that women usually went crazy about.

Now I understood why.

The thing was ... it might have started with attraction and some sense of safety, since he had saved me twice from demons, but I was sure it had evolved into more. Much more.

I really liked him, and I didn't know what to do about that, what to think of that.

So for now, I acted normal. Or tried to. I was sure he had caught me staring at him, at his handsome face and hot body, longer than what was polite. And I was sure my cheeks had turned bright red then.

But he never said anything about it. Which made me wonder. What was the deal? Was I a charity case he was using to repent for all the bad things he kept saying he had done in the past? Or was he really a good guy? Or ... could he be a little interested in me too?

I didn't delve into that too much, though, for fear of being disappointed.

For now, I preferred living in fantasyland and having one-sided feelings.

One late Thursday night, Rey escorted me back to the entrance of the female dorm, as he usually did after our practice.

He halted in front of the steps and turned to me. "You're doing well."

I wrinkled my nose. "Not as well as I should." I had been able to use and control darkfire for days now. Rey had even shown me some more complicated spells with it, like creating a wave of darkfire to push enemies back, but I still couldn't do other demonic spells. We had tried a few, but when I failed, Rey went back to the darkfire, probably so I wouldn't feel like such a failure.

"You are," he said. "As for the rest, you'll get it eventually. Don't worry."

But when? I had been living on the edge of my seat, waiting for some shadow or demon to jump out of every corner and attack me. I wanted to believe that this mark on my wrist would go away, as Rey had predicted, and no prince of the underworld would come for me, but even Rey, who worked directly with one of the princes, was worried about it. I probably should work harder to learn these damn spells.

"Right," I muttered, not feeling it.

"Hey," Rey said, taking a step toward me. I was standing on top of the first step leading to the dorm's front door, and he was on the ground. I was his height, and with him so close, only a foot from me, under the cover of the night, it felt intimate. "It's going to be okay. I won't let anything happen to you."

I held my breath as he stared into my eyes. Did he feel what I felt? Was his heart beating like a race car? Did he want to erase the distance between us and kiss me like I wanted to kiss him?

Answering me, his gaze flicked to my lips. "Erin, I—"

The sound of footsteps startled us. I took a step back, almost tripping on the stairs, and Rey turned to the incoming person.

"Tavin," he said, acknowledging the guard walking our way. "What can I help you with?"

"Actually, I'm here for Erin." He extended his hand and showed me a white envelope. "I was sent to deliver this to you."

Frowning, I took the envelope from him. "Thanks."

The guard marched away, and Rey approached me again. "What is it?"

I opened the envelope and fished out the sheet of paper inside.

Come see me in my office. Alone.

It wasn't signed, but I knew her handwriting. "It's from Professor Martha. She wants me to go see her in her office."

"Right now?" He glanced at his wristwatch. "It's midnight."

"I know," I said, a little worried. What could she want with me this late at night? Couldn't it wait until our next training session, which would be in exactly four hours.

"I'm going with you," Rey said.

I showed him the note. "You can't."

His brows slammed down. "I don't like this."

I reached for him and placed my hand on his chest. "Relax. Professor Martha knows about me and she hasn't turned me in yet. In fact, she has been training me harder because of it." His gaze dipped to my hand. I pulled it away. "Sorry," I mumbled, averting my face, so he wouldn't see my cheeks becoming red. Though it was dark here, he had told me that because of his demon blood, he could see well in the dark. He thought I could do the same thing, but so far, I either didn't have that ability, or I didn't know how to access it.

Rey let out a long breath. "Come on. I'll take you to the Aster building at least."

"You don't need to."

"I insist."

I walked toward the Aster building, my brain divided into two matters: Rey's protectiveness, which only enforced my wishful thinking that maybe he liked me too, and what the hell Professor Martha wanted.

Once more, he halted in front of the building and turned to me. "Want me to take you inside?"

I shook my head. "It's okay."

He crossed his arms. "I'll wait here."

"Rey," I said, fighting a smile. I kind of liked how alpha he was sometimes. "We don't know how long this will take. At least one of us should get some sleep."

"You think I'll be able to sleep while you're out and I don't know what's going on?"

Oh, my heart.

"I trust Professor Martha." For some odd reason. "Please, go. Rest for me." I batted my lashes at him.

His frown deepened. "You'll tell me tomorrow what she wanted with you, right?"

I nodded. "Of course I will."

"All right," he said with a sigh. "I'll leave once you go inside."

I started toward the door. "Good night."

"Good night," he muttered.

I entered the building and rounded the corner toward the staircase, but I halted once I was out of sight. I counted to ten, then spied at the entrance—standing exactly where I left him, Rey stared up at the building. Then, he shook his head once, turned around, and walked away.

I let out a relieved sigh. Seriously, I thought he wouldn't leave. I really wanted him to go sleep. Besides, one of us should.

Hoping this meeting was brief so I could also get to bed, I went to Professor Martha's office. I knocked on the closed door.

"Come in," she called from the inside.

I entered the office and closed the door beside me. "You called?"

"I did." She was seated behind her desk, her eyes on the computer screen on the corner. "Take a seat."

Shit, if she was asking me to sit down, it was because this conversation wouldn't be brief. Reluctantly, I took one of the two chairs across from her, and waited while she typed a few things.

I opened my mouth, but before any words came out, she turned and said, "Done. Sorry about that." She laced her fingers over her desk and looked at me. "Do you know why I called you here?"

I shook my head. "No, but at this time of the night, I'm guessing it's something urgent."

"It is," she said. A small knot appeared between her brows. "I saw you and Rey sneaking out of your dorms late last night." Oh, shit. "I followed you. You two have been training with your magic."

I inhaled sharply as worry snaked within me—worry for Rey. "Did you know about Rey?"

She nodded. "I did."

I frowned. "Who else knows?"

"As far as I know, only the headmaster, you, Harvey, and myself."

"Harvey?" I asked, confused.

"That's not what I wanted to talk to you about," she said. Her eyes softened a little. "Seeing you training with magic made me realize you're in more danger than I first thought. That you're trying to prepare for the terrible things coming, something I have been trying to avoid."

I shook my head. "I'm not following."

"Erin ... I don't think I can hide the truth from you anymore."

My chest clutched with dread. "What truth?"

Professor Martha let out a long breath. "I'm your mother."

I stared at her. I shook my head once and pressed my fingertips to my temple, but no matter what I did, her words rang inside my head. "I-I don't think I heard you right."

"My name is Martha Belmont, and my sister, Paula, changed her last name to Delman, so it would be harder to make the connection."

I blinked. "This ..." I didn't have any words.

"I know, this is a big surprise, but it's true," she said. "Your parents didn't die in an accident like Paula told you." My ears had to be playing a trick on me. "Before you were born, I was young and in love. I was a student at the academy, and I fell in love with a fellow demon hunter. Or so I thought. It turned out that this hunter was a higher demon in disguise. He was bidding his time, letting other demons enter the academy unnoticed. Until one night, he and his demons attacked us.

They slaughtered many students and brought chaos to the academy. Many did not survive." Her hazel eyes filled with tears. "I felt like an idiot because he had played me. He had used me, and I only realized that after it was too late. I felt horrible and guilty for how I had unknowingly betrayed everyone." She wiped at her unshed tears. "I went after the demon to kill him, but he was too strong for me, for anyone, for that matter. He got away."

I shook my head, because whatever she was telling me, sounded like a bad fairy tale. A work of fiction. It couldn't be true.

"A month later, I found out I was pregnant," she went on. "I knew you were his, of course, and because of that, a half-demon. If your father found out about it, he would claim you and take you to the underworld, and if the demon hunters found out, they would have killed you before you were even born." She swallowed hard. "So, I hid my pregnancy, and once you were born, I sent you away with Paula, who volunteered to keep you hidden and safe for as long as she could. Unfortunately, it wasn't as long as we both hoped."

I shot to my feet and paced in front of her desk. This was too much.

And nothing made sense.

Shit, my head hurt.

One thing poked in my mind and I grasped at it. If Aunt Paula was trying to hide me, why did she move so close to the academy?

"She moved with you to Canada first," Professor Martha answered my question. I stared at her. Had I said that out loud. "When you were little, you two moved around, because Paula was afraid of settling down. But as you got older, she wanted to provide you with a more stable life. That's why you didn't move as much. And when she finally decided to settle for good, she realized that being right under the enemies' noses would be best. If you were found out, everyone would assume she would have taken you far away."

I never knew ... I had hated moving so much and always gave Aunt Paula a terrible time because of that. Packing and unpacking was exhausting, and I could never make real friends when I wasn't sure how long we would stay in one place. Not that Aunt Paula had encouraged any of that. Our moving rate went significantly down once I turned ten. After that, we only moved two more times, closer and closer to Colorado.

"I stayed at the academy," Professor Martha said. "I stopped hunting, became a professor instead, and tried my best to keep informed of the demon activities in the area. If anything popped up, I warned Paula about it."

Now I understood why Aunt Paula had been so strict about making friends, going to regular school, going out, having a normal life.

If only I had known ...

What would have changed? I was a freaking teenager. I would have given her a terrible time no matter what.

And now, I regretted it so much.

"That's why I was shocked when I first saw you here, with Rey, no less," Professor Martha continued. "And that's also why I'm so hard on you. I need you to be prepared for when your father comes for you. Because he will. That mark on your wrist?" She pointed to my arm. "It's not a simple demon mark. It means you're the daughter of a powerful demon, and he'll do anything to drag you to the underworld. And now that you've shown that you inherited his powers, he'll probably come for you sooner."

I stopped pacing and faced her, my head spinning. "This is too much. I can't ... I can't make sense of anything. I need some space to think." To cry and yell and break something.

Professor Martha nodded. "I know it's a lot, but you're old enough to understand, and since I think things will only get worse from here, I thought it was time." She stood. "We can talk more about this later, if you wish, and if you have any questions, as I'm sure they will come, I'll be here to answer them."

I nodded, unable to find my voice. I grabbed the knob and she said, "Don't worry about training tomorrow morning. We'll skip it."

"Thanks," I muttered before opening the door and leaving her office.

My mother's office.

That was total bullshit.

I ran from the Aster building to the female dorm and into my room. I threw myself on my bed, hugged my pillow, and willed sleep to come.

But I was only met with tears.

* * *

I didn't sleep; I didn't rest. When morning came, I didn't eat breakfast, get ready, or go to class. I stayed in my room, numb to anything and everything.

My mother and my father were alive. They hadn't died in an accident. I should have been happy, right? But I wasn't. My mother was a demon hunter who looked down on me with disdain and pity, if not shame, and my father was supposedly a higher demon from the underworld. Probably a prince?

Like Prince Paimon? He was probably the reason why that general came to get me.

More demons would come, she said. Professor Martha didn't sound right anymore, but neither did the other word ...

Mother.

Nope, so not going there.

I inhaled, trying to calm down. But my mind wouldn't stop. If I wasn't agonizing over who my mother was, or about my father and the demons who would come for me, then I kept thinking about my life before I came to the academy. Was there anything real in my life? Besides the fact that Aunt Paula was really my aunt, was there anything else that was real? Did she really have a job that made her move around? Did she never marry because her fiancé had left her for another woman, and then she thought no man was worth it? Did she really dislike people, or was she reclusive because of me?

Maybe even my birthday and age were a lie.

Holy shit ...

A knock on the door startled me.

"Erin, are you there?" Claire asked.

I stared at the door. I could stay quiet and pretend I wasn't here. But maybe if I told Claire everything, she would make me see a positive side to all of this—even though I seriously doubted there was one.

She knocked again.

I stood up and unlocked the door. "Hey."

"Hey, girl, why didn't you come to—?" She stared at me with huge eyes. "Holy crap, what happened?" She looked me up and down. I still wore yesterday's clothes, probably super stinky, my hair a big rat's nest, with dark circles under my eyes. "Are you sick?"

I shook my head and it was like a faucet opened.

The tears came without warning.

"Oh, no." Claire stepped inside, closed the door behind her, and embraced me. "It's okay. Whatever it is, it's okay now."

She ran her hand up and down my back, trying to soothe me.

When I was able to stop crying, we sat down on the floor with our backs leaned against my bed, and I told her everything. About Professor Martha, my father, and my ill-fated destiny to be claimed and taken to the underworld against my will.

"I'm so sorry everything is so messed up," she said, her voice low and serene.

After I stopped crying, she brought fresh coffee and donuts from the cafeteria for us. I sipped my coffee, but I had no stomach to eat the donut, even if it smelled like heaven. I glanced at my friend over the cup. Were there really selfless and good-hearted people in the world like Claire, or was this a trick too? She had just met me, not even three months ago. I didn't understand why she was so accepting of my flaws and fate.

"Thanks for being there for me," I muttered, not sure what else to say.

She bumped her shoulder on mine. "That's what friends are for."

I wouldn't know; I had never had friends like her before. I let out a long breath. "I'm in some deep shit."

"Well, you should look on the bright side," Claire said. "One, if you're the daughter of a powerful demon, then it means your magic is powerful too. You can defend yourself better with it. And two, Professor Martha is one kickass hunter. She was willing to send you away to keep you safe. I can only imagine what else she'll do to make sure you stay safe."

"Let's *not* talk about her."

"No, I think that's one you have to talk about. Let it out, then be done with it."

My brows curled down. Could she be right? If I expelled all the feelings tangled in my chest, would I feel better after? "The mother I thought was dead is suddenly here, alive and well. I've been around her for almost three months now without any clue of who she was. She has been more like a commander in the army than a mother." I slapped my hands down on the floor. "How could she spend so much time with me and keep this huge secret to herself? Why did she treat me like I was a newbie cadet who couldn't do push-ups right?"

"She was trying to protect you—"

"Protect me? See how well that is going now? I would rather she had been there for me when I was growing up."

Claire nodded. "I know, believe me, I know. Ever since my mother died, I barely know my father. Worse, someone I barely know who actually expects me to be the best hunter ever born." She scoffed. "Sorry to disappoint you again, Dad. Not happening."

I snorted. "What a pair of parents we have."

"Maybe we should get them together," Claire joked. "They might actually make a good couple." We laughed at that. Shit, it was good to laugh because of something silly. "But joke aside, it would be nice to have you as a sister."

I laid my head on Claire's shoulders. "Right back at you."

After a short moment of silence when we drank more of

our coffee and ate our donuts—I finally surrendered to my hunger—Claire said, "So, what are we doing today?"

"You're going to class soon," I told her. "I'm gonna take the day off. I think I deserve it."

She shook her head. "Nu-uh. I'm staying with you."

I glanced at her, startled. "But you never skip classes."

"There's a first time for everything."

I smiled at her. "What did I do to deserve you?"

"Right back at you," she repeated my previous words.

In the end, we found the hidden movie room and watched a silly romantic comedy that made us roll with laughter—just the medicine I needed.

26

REY

Pacing around the clearing, I checked my wristwatch again. Erin was five minutes late. She had never been late for one of our training sessions before. Had some professor seen her out this late? But she had Professor Martha's pass. She should be able just to show them that and go on her way.

I started getting worried, and the coffee I had brought was getting cold.

Finally, I heard the crunch of grass as she approached the area. A moment later, Erin stepped into the clearing. The lantern I had set beside my books illuminated her just enough, showing me her eyes downcast.

"What's wrong?" I asked, walking to her.

"Sorry I'm late. I lost track of time. My mind isn't in the right place right now."

I offered her the coffee. "Want to talk about it?"

She took the paper cup, holding it with both hands, and let out a long breath. "Where to start?" She scoffed, something I had never heard her do before. "Remember Professor

Martha called me to her office last night? Yeah, it was to tell me she's my mother."

I stared at her. "What?"

She nodded. "If you're shocked, can you imagine how I feel?"

"Fuck," I muttered, wishing I had brought brandy instead of coffee. "How are you feeling?"

"I don't know, to be honest." She shrugged. "All my life I believed my parents had died in an accident when I was little. Then suddenly, I'm finding out one secret right after the other one. First, I'm a demon hunter, next I'm a half-demon, and that's why my aunt took me away from here. Then, my birth mother reveals herself and confirms that a higher demon is hunting me. What's next? I'll find out he promised my hand in marriage to another demon."

"Did Professor Martha tell you who your father is?" I asked, my voice low. Careful.

"No. She just said he's a powerful demon and he'll come for me. To join him in the underworld or whatever."

Prince Paimon had sent his most trusted general to get her, and he was a powerful demon. As a prince, he rivaled Asmodeus in power. If he was really the one after Erin, then we were screwed.

"It's okay," I told her. "That doesn't change our plans. You still have to prepare for what's coming."

"Right," she muttered. She sipped from her coffee. "I have to train."

She didn't sound eager to work on her magic. So, I decided to make it a little fun.

"I had an idea about the zombies you conjured during your magic spells class a couple of weeks ago." I dropped my coffee cup on the side of the clearing, over one of my books. "We can try that again."

She drank from her cup, then set it beside mine. "What do you mean?"

"You can summon zombie figures to distract your enemies. They might think they are real and try attacking them. That could give you an advantage."

We stood in front of each other in the center of the clearing. Erin rolled her shoulders. "Conjure the zombies again, but on purpose. Should be easy." There was a sarcastic tone to her voice.

I reached for her and took her hands in mine. Her eyes widened. "Just relax." I shook her arms, loosening her muscles. "You won't be able to conjure anything if tense."

She snorted. "Lately, I'm always tense."

I could understand why. "Forget everything else right now. Just look into my eyes, and think we're about to play a game." Her golden eyes burned into mine. Faint red spread over her cheeks. Fuck. During these past couple of weeks, while we trained alone under the night sky, there had been thousands of moments when all I wanted was to lean into her and kiss her. Right now was one of them. I cleared my throat and stepped back. "Ready?"

A small frown appeared between her brows as she nodded.

I asked her to replicate what she had done in Professor Martha's—her mother!—class.

"I was scared and upset," she said in a low voice. "I feel more confused and numb than scared right now."

"If you want to use that trick, you'll have to learn how to conjure it with any emotion you might feel," I told her. "Just focus and think about the zombies. Bring them to life."

It took her a few minutes and some tries, but Erin did it. She conjured zombies around the perimeter of the clearing —some of them shaped like vampires, others like werewolves, others like demons. I could even sense them, as if they were real.

Incredible.

Erin let out a shuddering breath. "What now?"

"Make them move," I told her. "As if they were real. That will throw your enemies off even more."

Her eyes narrowed. Erin groaned as she channeled her power. Slowly, the shadows started moving. Some were jerky, as if she was overthinking each of their movements, instead of letting it flow. But I didn't want to comment on each little thing. The important thing here was that she was doing it, and quite well for a first time too.

Following my instructions, Erin made the zombies advance toward us, then disappear in a dark cloud, making us blind for a moment. Then, I told her to summon them again and repeat the same process.

In the end, it hadn't been the fun game I had expected since she was still learning how to conjure and control them, but I was impressed with her progress. Erin was doing incredibly for someone who just found out she had powers not even twenty days ago.

She was incredible in every way.

Finally, after almost an hour practicing, Erin lay on the grass, breathing hard. "I'm done," she muttered. "I'm going to sleep right here tonight."

Chuckling, I approached her. A thin sheen of perspiration lined her forehead, and her chest moved up and down fast, but other than that, she was fine. More than fine.

An urge to lie over her hit me square in the chest, and I had to avert my eyes before I lost control.

The sound of footfalls approached. Erin sat up and I turned around, channeling my magic, ready to strike whoever was coming our way.

Holding a flashlight and a thick book, Claire stepped into the clearing. "Hey, it's just me."

"Claire?" Erin stood up. "What are you doing here?"

"After I started reading my father's books, I couldn't stop." She approached us. "I've read some interesting and weird stories in books that are probably forbidden to most of us. My father doesn't know I've been reading them, of course." She opened the book in her hands. "Anyway, I read about this and thought I should share it with you." She turned the book to us and pointed the flashlight to the page. "Here."

Erin and I leaned over the book.

The paragraph Claire had pointed to told about demonic portals—like magical doors—where demons could easily come through. There was a huge list of the known doors, and one of them was near here.

"Did you know about this?" Erin asked me. She knew I served Asmodeus, which meant I should know about everything that went on in the underworld.

Wrong.

I shook my head. "I've heard about the portals before, but I always thought they were myths."

"Turns out, most of the myths are actually true," Claire said. "Or at least, some parts of the myth." She flipped some pages in the book. "I wanted to show you this because I thought we could shut the portal." She pointed the flashlight to another paragraph. It explained a complicated ritual to close the portals. "If we close the portal, then it will be harder for the demons to get close to the academy." She stared at Erin. "And you'll be safer. I mean, everyone will, but ..." She didn't finish. She didn't need to. I knew what Claire meant, because I felt the same. If I could, I would do anything to keep Erin safe.

I frowned and thought for a moment. I had already battled and killed—along with Erin, Claire, and Ava—one famous general of Prince Paimon's army. Now, I would shut down a portal. Asmodeus would know something was up soon. He would summon me and demand an explanation. He would threaten to send me back to the underworld if I didn't fix things.

But I didn't care. As long as I was able to keep Erin safe, I would take whatever punishment that came my way.

"Let's do it," I said, confident about this plan. "Let's close the portal."

Erin stared at me. "Are you sure?"

I nodded. "Like Claire said, without the portal, demons won't be able to get close to the academy." All the demons that had sneaked in here these past couple of months ... I bet they had used that fucking portal. "Much less hurt you or anyone else."

Erin held my gaze for a moment, her golden eyes shining in the dark. "All right," she said in a low voice. "Let's do it."

"Right now?" Claire almost shrieked.

I glanced at my wristwatch. "It's late now and we need to gather the supplies for the ritual. Let's meet here tomorrow, at the usual time, then we go from here to the portal."

Claire hugged the closed book. "I'll make a list of supplies and get them. I'll let you know if I can't find anything."

After confirming our plan, we walked back to the dorms. I

dropped the girls in front of the female dorm. Erin lingered a few extra seconds.

"Good night," she whispered.

"Night." I waved at her.

I watched until she disappeared inside the building and the lights in her room came on. Then, I headed to my dorm, where I didn't sleep well—my dreams were plagued by a nightmare of all the princes of the underworld invading the academy and taking Erin away.

*　*　*

AFTER A BAD NIGHT, I WOKE UP IN A BAD MOOD. THE ONLY thing that got me through the day was knowing I would meet Erin later and we would do something to increase her chances against her mysterious, powerful father.

I hadn't heard from Claire, so I assumed she had been able to gather all the supplies needed for the ritual. I got three cups of coffee from the cafeteria before heading out to the clearing that night.

In my eagerness to get this done, I ended up in the clearing earlier than usual. Which meant I would have to wait longer for Erin and Claire, and the coffee was sure to get fucking cold.

I sipped from my coffee as the tug in my mind started.

What the fuck?

I left the paper cups at the roots of a tree, where it was flatter, then I shapeshifted into my raven and flew above the academy's outer walls. In five minutes, I arrived at the entrance to a cave at the base of the mountain—the portal was here.

Asmodeus smiled at me. "I thought you wouldn't come."

I did my best not to glare at him. "What are you doing here?"

"Is that any way to speak to your father?" His amused expression faded. "To your owner?"

Rage simmered in my veins. "You've never cared about how I talked to you."

"Some things change," he said through gritted teeth. "Like my patience. It's volatile. And right now, I'm all out of it."

"What do you mean?"

"You haven't killed Randall yet, as I ordered." He extended his hand to me. "So, I'm here to do something about it."

A jet of darkfire flew at me. I dodged it, only to be hit with another strike, right in the chest. The amount of power Asmodeus had infused in his hit was enough to bring me to my knees.

"What are you doing?" I croaked, fighting through the pain, through the tremors that overtook every inch of me, through the numbness that followed.

"You shall see." He sent another strike.

It hit me in the chest again. Excruciating pain flashed before the darkness washed over me, taking me under.

27

I WAS THE FIRST TO ARRIVE AT OUR MEETING PLACE, WHICH WAS odd because Rey had always been here first, waiting for me with coffee or hot chocolate, or both. In the dark, I stood in the middle of the clearing and waited.

A few minutes passed. No sign of Rey or Claire. Shit, how I wanted to be able to carry my cell phone around. It would be easy to just call them right now and ask what the holdup was. But cell phones were forbidden at the academy. We could have them in our dorms, but we weren't supposed to use them too much, especially not for social media.

I waited a little longer.

Finally, almost thirty minutes later, Claire ran into the clearing. "Thank goodness, you're still here," she said, out of breath. "I thought you two would be long gone by now."

As if we would go anywhere without her. "What happened?" I asked.

"I was caught sneaking out of the house by my father. Thankfully, he didn't see the books I was borrowing." She gestured to her backpack, hanging down heavily on her back. Frowning, she glanced around. "Where's Rey?"

"I don't know," I said, starting to worry for real. "It's not like him to be this late."

"Do you think he was also held up by something? Maybe he's running some errand from the headmaster."

There was no way of knowing. "Why don't we walk around the campus and look for him?"

"It's past curfew," Claire reminded me. "What if we're caught?"

I showed her the pass from Professor Martha—I still refused to call her anything else. "I always carry it with me, just in case."

"She didn't give you that so you could sneak around the academy. You know that, right?"

I shrugged. "She doesn't need to know. Let's go."

We went back to the stone paths between the buildings and walked around, hoping to find Rey somewhere. We stopped in front of the Snapdragon building and watched his window—it was dark. Where the hell could he be?

"I don't want to."

Claire and I whipped in the direction of the new voice. Harvey and Ava walked toward the dorms.

"But you didn't even hear me," Ava said, leaning into Harvey.

He took a large step to the side. "Ava, just stop."

Ava reached to him, but then she saw us and her steps faltered.

Harvey, on the other hand, smiled at us. "Hello, ladies." He halted right in front of me. "What brings you two out at this time?"

Ava halted beside Harvey, her arms crossed. "You know it's past curfew, right?"

I frowned. Whatever they were doing, wherever they were coming from, I didn't care, but she just had to push first. "I can tell you the same thing."

She flipped her hair over her shoulder. "It's none of your business."

I considered ignoring them and continuing our search, but they were coming from somewhere on campus. They could have seen Rey. "We're looking for Rey," I told them. "Have you seen him?"

Harvey's brows curled down. "I thought I told you to stay away from him."

Ava humphed.

"You did, but I didn't listen," I said, trying not to sound like a bitch and failing. I tried again. "Please, this is important."

Harvey let out a long breath. "I saw him going that way earlier." He pointed to the corner where our training clearing was.

My eyes widened. "Do you remember when exactly?"

He glanced to his wristwatch. "Almost an hour ago, I think."

One hour ago? Then he should have been there. But he hadn't been there. With one thought in mind, I marched back to the clearing, barely aware that Claire, Harvey, and Ava followed me.

I stepped into the dark clearing and looked around. Rey was the one who always brought flashlights. I could barely see the silhouette of the trees around the clearing like this.

"Here," Claire said, turning on a flashlight. I stared at her.

She shrugged. "What? I thought we would need it ... for later."

I took one of the flashlights from her and started looking around. She turned on another and did the same.

"What are you looking for?" Ava asked.

"Rey," Claire answered.

"I bet you would be able to see him without a flashlight," Ava said. "Or you can call him. Rey!"

"If that was the case, then we would have found him already," I said, my eyes trained on the trees the flashlight illuminated.

"Oh no," Claire muttered.

I froze. "What is it?"

She pointed her flashlight to the roots of a tree. A paper tray stood there with three paper cups. "I think he was here."

My stomach tightened. "Then ... where is he?" Something had happened, something bad. I just knew it. I felt it deep inside me. "We need to find him," I said, forcing my muscles to move again. "Right now."

"What's going on?" Ava asked.

"You think something happened to Rey?" Harvey asked, his voice tight.

"I do." I nodded, sure of it. "We need to find him. Claire, let's separate and go around the outer walls, and—"

"I can help," Harvey said. I stared at him, a little wary.

Ava straightened. "Me too."

I frowned at her. I was sure she was just saying that because Harvey had volunteered. Otherwise, she would have bid us good night and marched away, without a care in the world.

"We might not need to look for him." Claire dropped her flashlight and her backpack on the ground. She fished a small notebook from inside the backpack, her eyes on me. "We might be able to cast a tracking spell."

"Cast a spell?" Ava snorted. "We aren't witches, Claire. We can't cast spells."

I knew what Claire meant. They couldn't cast spells, but I could. But for that, I would have to reveal my identity to Harvey and Ava. I hesitated for a second, but really, I shouldn't have. If this was to find Rey, I would tell the whole academy about me.

It wasn't easy though. Inhaling deeply, I turned to Harvey and Ava. "I might be able to cast the tracking spell."

Ava wrinkled her nose and said, "That doesn't make any sense."

Harvey's eyes went wide with understanding. "You're like him."

I nodded. "A half-demon, yes." Not really caring about their reactions or opinions, I turned back to Claire. "Show me the spell."

She handed me the notebook. I flipped through it, noting the many spells she had copied from the books we had researched. "Someone has been busy."

She offered me a small smile. "I like reading and studying. I can't resist a mysterious book, and there are way too many of them in my father's office."

It was good, though. If she hadn't developed this new hobby, we wouldn't know how to start looking for Rey. Now, we only needed this spell to work.

I found the spell and read through it. It didn't seem difficult and didn't need many things, the worst item being something that had belonged to Rey. I picked up the tray with the coffee cups and checked the one with less coffee in it. He must have drunk it while he waited for us.

I followed the spell's direction: channel my power, think of Rey while holding the cup, and send my magic into it. I confess I was a little skeptical, but before I knew it, I felt it. It was like a tug inside my chest, pulling me forward.

"I think it worked," I whispered, rising to my feet. "I can feel it."

"All we have to do is follow it," Claire said. She picked up her notebook, stuffed it inside her backpack, and swung it over her shoulders. "Let's go."

Harvey took a step forward. "I'm coming too."

I shook my head. "I can't let you guys get more involved in this. Just go back to your dorm and pretend you didn't see us."

He shook his head. "No matter what you say, I'm coming. You can't stop me."

Ava watched Harvey with indignant eyes, then sighed. "Fine. I'm coming too."

What the—?

"All right," I relented, because the tug was strong, increasing the sense of urgency within me. I didn't want to waste time. "Let's go."

28

———————

REY

I woke up with a gasp, as if I had been underwater. My desperation only increased when I realized I couldn't move my arms and legs. "What the fuck?" I muttered, trying to get my bearings. I was tied to a tombstone in an abandoned graveyard.

Asmodeus was seated on another tombstone a few feet from me, a wide smile on his lips. "Finally, the damsel in distress is awake. I didn't even hit you that hard."

I jerked against the chains, but I knew there was no chance I was escaping. These dark chains were enchanted with old, dark magic, stronger than mine.

Recalling what he had said before attacking me, I said, "You gave me until the end of the semester to kill Randall. I still have time. Release me and let me do it."

Asmodeus lost his smile. "If you were going to honor our deal, you would have done it by now."

I shook my head. "That's not true. I needed to get close to him to learn his weaknesses. That takes time."

"Just another excuse."

"You know I'm not strong enough to face him and simply kill him," I said. "I need to find out a weakness, a good one, otherwise I'll die at his hands, and he'll keep tormenting your nightmares."

Asmodeus balled his hands into fists for a moment. One thing I had always admired him for was, despite his volatile demon temper, he was actually good at controlling his actions and having patience.

His smile came back. "Did you know that demons can take the lives of their offspring and absorb their magic to become even more powerful?"

I stared at him. Of course I knew that, but if he was saying that to intimidate me, he would be disappointed. "So that's your plan? To kill me and absorb my powers?"

"I'll confess that it makes me a little sad," he said nonchalantly. "I've become attached to you after having you around for so long. I never had a better servant, but all good things must come to an end."

"Then do it," I said through gritted teeth.

I wouldn't succumb to his luring, but it didn't mean I was happy about it. For many, many years, I hadn't care if I lived or died. I was a walking zombie, doing whatever was requested of me. But now ... now I wanted to live. I had someone to protect.

He tilted his head. "Aren't you curious why I'm willing to kill you?"

I shook my head once. "Don't care."

"What a disappointment." Asmodeus tsked. A small black dagger appeared in his hand. He slashed his palm and black blood dripped to the ground. "With your powers, I'll be able to kill Randall myself." He squeezed his hand, making more blood drip. Then, he walked around me, marking a circle in the grass with his blood. "If I kill him, then I'll be honored by King Brikan. Who knows, maybe he'll even favor me more than Prince Paimon."

Prince Paimon. He was the one after Erin. King Brikan's favorite prince.

Before I could think more about it, or even ask my father if he knew something about Prince Paimon these days, Asmodeus closed the circle and stalked to me.

In one swift motion, Asmodeus swung the dagger down, slicing my chest open. I screamed as the pain burned and tormented every one of my cells and nerves. Dark red blood poured from the cut, soaking my shirt and stomach.

Lightheaded, I blinked fast, trying to stay awake.

"Don't fight it," Asmodeus said. "It'll only hurt more if you do."

I blinked again, but all I saw was black.

Pure black.

Then, a faint light flickered beside me. I glanced at the candle's flame.

"Shh," someone said, scooting closer to me. A little girl glanced up at me. "Do you think she heard us?"

I stared at my little girl, too shocked to think.

Marian. My sister.

Footsteps sounded from the hallway outside our room.

"She's coming." Marian blew out on the candle.

Darkness enveloped us for a moment.

Then, the door opened and a woman holding a candle spied into the room. "I know you two were reading. I already told you it's late. Please, just go to sleep. You can read tomorrow."

I stared, transfixed at the woman in the doorway.

My mother.

Marian sat up on her bed. "But Mother, we're almost at the end. We need to know what happens next."

My mother smiled. She turned her blue eyes at me. "Reyan, tell her, she can finish it tomorrow." I couldn't say anything. The words didn't come. "As the oldest, I trust you. Don't read to her anymore. Now, back to bed."

She blew us a kiss, then exited the room, closing the door behind her. Darkness washed over us.

When light reappeared, I was once again paralyzed. My mother and my sister lay together in bed, both too pale and thin, with dark, sunken eyes, and coughing up blood.

Plague. They had the plague.

"Go, Reyan," my mother urged between coughs. "Leave before you catch it. Please."

The room, my mother and sister, even the darkness melted away, giving way to the edge of a forest. A tall man with long, blond hair stood before me.

"Asmodeus," I whispered, remembering this. It had been when he came to me, knowing I would take a deal this time. When I finally sold my soul to him to save my mother and my sister.

"You remember now?" he asked, more serious than usual. "Do you regret it?"

It? The deal? I swallowed hard. "No." It was the truth. Because I had made a deal with him, my mother and my sister were healed and went on to live long, happy lives.

Lives where I had never existed.

"Don't worry," Asmodeus said. "You'll finally be able to join them." That didn't sound bad. Not bad at all. "Just close your eyes."

I did. Darkness welcomed me again.

I was dying.

It was okay, though.

I would soon be at peace.

A scream pierced my dream and my eyes shot open.

No, no, fucking no.

Erin, Claire, Harvey, and Ava ran into the cemetery, their Dawnblades raised to defend against Asmodeus.

Erin took a step forward and glared at the demon. "Stay away from him!"

29

ERIN

IT WAS TRUE. I WAS SHAKING ON THE INSIDE, BUT I TRIED NOT to think about it. I focused on the fear I felt over seeing Rey chained to the tombstone, the deep cut across his chest, his pale skin, and the incredible amount of blood pooling around him. I also focused on the rage I felt for the demon who had done this to him.

I pointed my aunt's Dawnblade at the demon. "Stay away from him!" I shouted, sounding braver than I was.

Ever since performing the tracking spell and following it, I had felt braver. Before leaving the academy, I went back to the dorms and grabbed my aunt's sword. Since Claire, Harvey, and Ava already had made theirs, they could summon it at will. Next, I used the pass from Professor Martha to leave the grounds like I had done before. The guard probably heard about the previous time, because he didn't want to let us pass, but when I threatened to call the professor, to wake her up to deal with something so trivial, he relented.

I followed the tug through the forest, with Claire, Harvey,

and Ava right behind me. We practically jogged past the trees and down to the base of the mountain for over two hours, until we reached a small, abandoned town I didn't even know existed.

The pull didn't ease until we arrived at a crumbling church and the cemetery beside it.

When I saw Rey ... a pang cut through my chest.

Holy shit ... if he died, this demon was toast.

This demon.

I was sure this was Asmodeus, Rey's father. For some reason, he was ritualistically sacrificing Rey. But I would stop him. Somehow, I would stop him.

"Erin, no ... no," Rey croaked, his words broken. I didn't dare take my eyes from the demon.

Asmodeus let out a long laugh. "What if I don't?"

"Then I'll have to kill you," I said. Later, I would chastise myself for being so freaking stupid and talking to a prince of the underworld like that.

A sly smile stretched over his pale lips. "I would like to see you try."

My pleasure, I thought as I channeled my power.

Like Rey had instructed me, I conjured zombies from the edges of the cemetery—zombified versions of demons, fae, werewolves, and vampires—and sent them toward Asmodeus.

Watching the zombies with mild interest, Asmodeus didn't see as Claire opened a book, in search of a spell to stun him, or Harvey and Ava, who sneaked through the forest, going for Rey.

Or so I thought.

With one flick of his hands, Asmodeus had Harvey and Ava and Claire against tombstones, trapped like Rey. Dark vines sprouted from the ground and wound over their legs and arms. Ava screamed—a vine wound around her mouth too.

"It's just you and me," Asmodeus said, taunting me.

I knew I was no match for a prince, but I would be damned if I didn't try my best to at least injure him enough so I could get Rey and my friends and flee.

Rolling my shoulders, I tried to remember all my fighting lessons with Professor Martha. Feet apart, shoulders relaxed, hands tight, core braced. Be vigilant and aware of the surroundings, and expect the unexpected.

I didn't wait for him to come to me. I sent my zombies to the demon prince. They closed in around him, while I rushed him.

With a roar, the demon sent a powerful wave out, clearing out all my zombies. But by then, I was within range. I swung my sword wide, but the demon stepped back.

He chuckled. "Not bad."

I sent a ray of darkfire at him. Asmodeus whipped his shoulders and deflected it, but then I was coming down with the Dawnblade. The sword cut through his upper arm.

Asmodeus's eyes turned black and he let out a howl. "You insolent girl." In the blink of an eye, Asmodeus took the Dawnblade from me and brought it down over me. I stumbled back, but not before the tip of the sword cut my tee, from my shoulder to my chest. I didn't dare breathe, afraid of any pain if it had cut my skin.

But none came. Maybe my adrenaline was too high and I couldn't feel it yet.

I did feel when he waved his hand and a burst of magic hit me in the chest, sending me flying back. I landed hard against a tombstone, my head and back screaming in pain.

Then, vines shot up from the ground and wound around my legs and arms.

"No, no!" I screamed, jerking against them.

"You can't fight it," Asmodeus said. He threw my aunt's Dawnblade away and walked toward me.

I wracked my brain, looking for a way out of this mess. But what came to mind wasn't an escape plan but a realization. When we summoned the demon behind my mark, General Verin came forward. He had been under Prince Paimon, Rey had told us. But the prince smiling at me right now as if he had finally gotten his prize was Asmodeus. Could Verin have been working for Asmodeus instead? Or Prince Paimon and Asmodeus were working together?

Asmodeus knelt in front of me. The blood drained from my face.

I wouldn't show him my fear, though. I jerked against the vines again. "I can try."

He shook his head, his long, blond hair immobile. "You'll exhaust yourself." Then, he shrugged. "Which wouldn't be a bad idea. Go ahead. Fight. You'll give up soon enough."

The desperation inside me spiked, but I tried surrounding it with anger. "Then get this shit over with and kill me!"

"No!" Rey shouted. Even though I didn't dare look at him again, it was good to know he was still awake.

"Kill you?" Asmodeus tilted his head. "I don't want to kill you. I want to capture you."

I inhaled a sharp breath. "I would rather die than go to the underworld with you."

"I'm afraid you have no choice." His smile widened. "You are a demonic princess, Erin. You're the daughter of King

Brikan, and because of that, you are set to inherit the throne of the underworld."

I stared at him, sure I was either hearing nonsense, or he was high and fabricating crazy stories. "No way," I whispered.

"Those girls, Brianne and Cindy? They were also demonic princesses. Your half-sisters," he continued, shocking me more. "King Brikan was playing three different women at once at the academy, and one of them was Martha, your mother. He created three daughters, so when they came of age and inherited his powers, he could kill them and absorb their powers to become even stronger. That way, King Brikan is sure to accomplish his goal of enslaving all the demon hunters and dominating the entire world."

I shook my head, because ... this was impossible. Me, a demonic princess? Daughter of the king of the underworld? It sounded like a terrible D-rated movie.

"If I deliver you to the king personally," he went on, "I'll be hailed a hero. With you in my arms, and Reyan's powers in my veins, I'm sure to gain his ultimate favor."

I swallowed hard. All of this sounded insane, but at the same time, I knew Asmodeus wasn't lying. Why would he? Any plan of escaping fled my mind. I couldn't escape from this. Even if I managed to leave this place and go back to the academy, I was the daughter of the freaking king of the underworld. How did I escape that?

I couldn't save myself, but perhaps I could save the others. Claire, Harvey, Ava, and Rey.

"All right." I inhaled deeply. "I'll go with you." My friends' protests rang loud, but I tuned them out. "But only if you leave them alone. Including Rey."

Asmodeus looked at them from over his shoulder. He seemed to consider it for a moment. He turned his wicked eyes to me. "I accept." Some of the vines around me retreated, leaving only my wrists and ankles tied. Asmodeus curled his fingers, as if calling me to him, and an invisible force pushed me off the tombstone, until I was standing in front of him. The demon closed his cold hand around my upper arm. "This should be fun."

"Erin, no, don't do this," Rey said, his voice a raspy whisper. Finally, I glanced in his direction. He was even paler than before, and the amount of blood around him ... my stomach knotted.

Asmodeus hesitated, his eyes on Rey. "I've changed my mind," he said. "I'll leave your friends alone, but not Reyan." Darkfire appeared in his hand and he threw it at Rey.

"No!" I cried.

The darkfire struck Rey's chest. His body jerked and his head lolled forward.

My heart stopped.

"Now, I can have his powers." Asmodeus lifted his free hand. I felt his magic brushing against my skin as it traveled toward Rey.

I had to do something, anything, but his grip on me was tight, and the vines around my wrists and ankles were too powerful for me.

"Stop this madness!"

I whipped my head at her voice. Professor Martha stood at the entrance of the cemetery—headmaster Randall by her side.

Asmodeus's magic faded, his grip on me loosened, and his face turned pale.

"Long time no see," the headmaster said as he walked forward as if he was taking a leisurely stroll through the park.

Letting go of me, Asmodeus took a step back. "What are you doing here?"

Randall gestured to my friends and me. "You've got my students. I've come to take them back to the academy."

Asmodeus puffed his chest. "Over my dead body."

Randall tsked. "So be it."

A sword like the Dawnblade appeared in his hand, but it seemed cruder, made of old wood. Still, a dark glow surrounded its blade. In a flash, Randall leaped and appeared right in front of Asmodeus.

Professor Martha's hands closed around my shoulders and she pulled me back, out of the way of the battle.

I stared, transfixed, as Randall and Asmodeus fought—one with dark magic, the other with his enchanted weapon.

Asmodeus sent several rays of darkfire toward Randall. The headmaster swung his sword, deflecting them all. In a fast spin, he caught up with the demon again. He brought his blade down—it would have split Asmodeus's head open if the demon hadn't cast a darkfire shield.

But the moment the sword hit the shield, it broke, the force of the impact pushing them apart a few feet.

They were at each other's throats again. Their movements, their strikes, their precision—it was rather graceful. Masterful. Two brilliant opponents in a heated battle.

Professor Martha cut the vines around my wrists and ankles with her Dawnblade. I rubbed against my sore skin. "Let's free the others," she told me, before rushing to Ava.

I glanced at Claire, then at Harvey. They were bound, but well.

I ran to Rey.

"Rey, Rey." I knelt beside him, getting my feet and knees

soaked in his blood. "Please, answer me." I cupped his face and forced it up. "Please, don't die."

His eyes fluttered open. "Erin," he whispered.

Tears filled my eyes. He wasn't dead! "Yes, it's me." I tugged on the chains around him. Why wasn't he tied with vines like I had been? Because he probably could break free easily from those. "Please, hang on. I'll take care of you." Remembering my aunt's Dawnblade, I looked around. The sword was a few feet from Randall and Asmodeus's feet. "Shit," I whispered.

I wouldn't be able to break the chains without the blade, and to take Rey out of here, to the infirmary or a hospital or anywhere someone could save him, I needed to cut him off the tombstone.

I watched the fight for a moment. Asmodeus sent a wave of darkfire at Randall, who once again moved his sword down, ripping through it as if it were smoke—how did he do that? His sword poised, Randall leaped at Asmodeus. The demon caught the blade high and the two of them struggled for power.

That was my chance. I ran toward them, crouched down, and grabbed the Dawnblade, a couple of feet from where they were standing.

I started to turn.

Asmodeus saw me. With renewed energy, he pushed Randall back, then lunged for me. With a yelp, I jumped out of his reach but was caught on a tall headstone jutting up from the grass. His hands grazed my throat.

Then Randall's Dawnblade was inches from my face. He cut off Asmodeus's hands, before swinging the sword back and cutting the demon across the chest. Screaming,

Asmodeus stumbled back. Randall plunged the blade into the demon's heart.

Asmodeus's eyes widened, his mouth fell open. Black rays flashed from the Dawnblade into the demon's body. When Randall pulled the sword out, Asmodeus crumbled to the ground. He twitched a couple of times. Then, his body exploded in a dark cloud of smoke.

Rey! Holy shit, Rey.

With the Dawnblade in my hands, I went back to Rey. I cut the chains around him, and his torso slumped over mine. I wound my arms around him, holding him so he wouldn't fall to the ground.

"Hang on," I told him, wishing we were closer to the academy. Wishing I had a purer kind of magic so I could heal him. "Please, hang on. You'll be fine."

"Liar," he whispered. He looked up at me. "It's okay. At least you're safe now."

A tear rolled down my cheek. He was dying and worried about my safety. Many feelings choked me—rage, fear, hope, love—and I just acted on them.

I leaned into Rey and kissed him.

30

WHEN ERIN'S LIPS MET MINE, I THOUGHT I HAD DIED AND GONE to heaven. But that was impossible. In my long life, I had done many, many terrible things. Even if I performed the most merciful of acts, I would never go to heaven.

The underworld was my home and would always be.

But for a moment, I moved my lips against Erin's, savoring her sweet taste, relishing in her alluring rose scent, grateful for this little piece of heaven.

Though I would have loved to kiss her longer, or even many times after this, I knew my time on this Earth was ending. I could feel my spirit slipping away.

I reached up and entwined my hand in her hair. Fuck, how I wished I had told her how I felt about her. I wished I had spent more time with her, seen her smile more.

Kissed her.

The strength in my body gave away. My arm dropped and I pulled back, wanting to look into those beautiful golden eyes one last time.

But Erin turned her head away from me. "Please, Head-master Randall, do something. Please, save him."

"He can't," Professor Martha said. She was standing directly behind the headmaster, with Claire, Harvey, and Ava beside her.

"Actually, I can," Randall said. He approached us. "I can save him, but everything has a price, Erin. If Rey wants to live, he'll have to be bound to me for eternity."

What the fuck? Another contract, but this time with Randall? I shook my head. "No, I won't do it."

Finally, those golden eyes turned to me, a desperate shine in them. "Please, Rey. Please, take it." Her fingers curled into my skin. "I don't want you to die. Please, stay with me."

Those eyes, that voice, that touch. I didn't want any more bargains with my soul, but how could I resist when Erin was begging me?

"Fine," I muttered, my voice hurting in my throat.

Randall knelt beside me. He put a hand over my chest. His magic poured into me. Slowly, it closed the wound in my chest, not even leaving a scar behind. I knew he was powerful and had magic—something no other pure demon hunter had —but I had no idea he could bring someone back from the brink of death.

"Done," he said. "Now you're mine for eternity. Or until I let you go." I cringed as the biding magic flowed into my veins. I knew that he would never let me go. Any hope would only lead to more disappointment. Randall unfolded to his feet. "You'll still feel weak and dizzy for another day or so. Take it easy."

My spirit was safe, my body had been restored back to its original state, but like Randall said, I was weak to the point where I could lay here and sleep for an entire year.

Groaning, I sat up straighter, freeing Erin from having to hold me. I glanced at her, at the beautiful girl with her pants soaked in my blood, and her torn shirt. I frowned, noticing the small, black tattoo an inch above her heart. It looked like two hearts entwined, plus some other swirly lines.

"Thank you," Erin said, taking my attention away from her tattoo. Her eyes still shone with tears.

"Don't thank me yet," Randall said to her. "I know you're also a half-demon, daughter of the Supreme Demon. I won't expose your secret if you're willing to bargain with me."

"What?" Bargaining with me wasn't enough? He had to go for Erin too. "No!"

Erin sucked in a sharp breath. "What is the bargain?"

"I'll keep your secret, and in addition, I'll keep you safe from your father. For that, you have to work for me too."

"No!" I protested.

Professor Martha touched Erin's shoulder. "You should accept it." What? She wasn't really saying that, was she? "Randall is powerful and has the demon hunters' best interest at heart. He'll keep your secret safe. He'll keep *you* safe. Please, Erin, accept the deal."

Erin's brows curled down as she considered it. I wanted to tell her that no, that even though I didn't have proof, Randall didn't seem like a good person. She shouldn't have her soul attached to him. But I didn't dare open my mouth in front of him, lest he decided to terminate our contract right now and let me die.

Now that he was taking Erin under his wing, I wanted to stay alive and well so I could protect her, from all the demons who would come for her—and from him too.

Finally, Erin sighed. "I accept." She gasped as the binding magic rushed through her.

Fuck. It was done.

Randall turned to the others. "As for you all, if you don't want to be expelled from the academy and punished severely, forget everything you saw here tonight."

Claire, Harvey, and Ava muttered their agreements. Randall nodded, then marched away.

"Let's go back to the academy," Professor Martha said, ushering everyone out of the cemetery.

Erin held on to my arms and helped me up.

"I'm fin—" I had to shut my mouth when a wave of dizziness came over me.

Erin's grip tightened. "You're not fine."

"I will be." I disentangled myself from her.

She lowered her gaze. "Sorry about your deal. I know it was probably the last thing you wanted. Having your soul belong to someone else seconds after you were finally free."

"It's not your fault."

She lifted her eyes to me. Tears brimmed in them. "Yes, it is. If I hadn't begged, you would have—" She pressed her lips tight. She wiped at the tears before they could fall. "I'm sorry, but I don't regret it. I couldn't bear the thought of you ... dead."

If my heart could rip in two, it would.

Professor Martha called us again. Reluctantly, Erin and I joined the others. While we rode back to the academy in a black SUV, Professor Martha gave us a lecture—about how foolish we had been, thinking we could defeat a prince of the underworld by ourselves, about not doing something like that ever again if we didn't want to face dire consequences, about keeping quiet and pretending nothing ever happened.

After the lecture, Ava humphed. "I knew you were trouble." She glanced at Erin. "The moment you arrived at the academy, I knew it. I'll keep quiet, but that doesn't mean I have to like this. I hate that you dragged me into all of this."

"Hey, you weren't dragged," Harvey protested.

"Right," Claire said. "You could have stayed behind. You're the one who wanted in."

"It doesn't matter," Ava said. "It's all because of Erin."

Meanwhile, Erin stared out of the window, her hands balled into fists as if she was trying hard not to rebuke.

"All of you, shut up," Professor Martha snapped from the front. "If I hear one more voice, you're all spending the night cleaning the Hyacinth building."

Everyone quieted down at once.

Back at the academy, Randall disappeared into the Aster building, but Professor Martha escorted us back to our rooms. She dropped the girls at the Gardenia building entrance, then moved on to the Snapdragon building.

After watching Harvey and I enter the building, Professor Martha finally left.

At the stairs, Harvey turned to me. "I'm sorry about your father." His voice was low and he was avoiding my gaze, but I knew he meant it. "And sorry about your deal with Randall."

I nodded. To be honest, I wasn't sure how I felt about my father. He had never been a father, just a demon who owned my soul and ordered me around. He had been evil. Despicable.

Actually, I knew how I felt about his death.

Relieved.

Now, the deal with Randall ... that was fucking terrible and even I felt sorry for myself.

"I'll be fine," I assured him.

Harvey nodded. "I know you will. Well, good night." He climbed the stairs and headed to his room.

I hesitated, tired but at the same time too wound up to lie down and rest.

"Rey."

I turned toward the low voice. Erin entered the Snapdragon building. "What are you doing here?"

"I wanted to check on you," she said, her eyes rummaging over me. "If you're fine."

"I'm fine," I told her. It seemed I would be saying that a lot for the next couple of days. "You should go."

"I ... " She frowned.

"What is it?"

She shook her head. "I thought ..."

I knew what she thought. We had kissed. I had clung to her so desperately, taking in every drop of herself that she would give me, sure I was dying. But then I wasn't, and I realized that even though I wanted to keep her safe, that I would keep her safe, she wouldn't be safe with me.

Besides my terrible past, I now had a deal with Randall, and I was sure this deal would force me to do more terrible things. Worse things. Things that would make her hate me if she found out about them.

Erin thought I liked her.

She wasn't wrong, but she could never know.

Moreover, Randall could never know. If he found out she liked me and I liked her, he would exploit it. I couldn't let him have another angle to hurt us, to hurt her.

"About the kiss," I started, bracing myself for the whiplash of my words. "Sorry about that. I was dying and you kissed me first. It was nice, but ... I'm okay now."

Her eyes widened. "Oh."

"Yeah, it was fun, but that was just it."

Her shoulders drooped. "You mean ..."

Fuck, I couldn't say it. I couldn't be so mean to her. *Please, Erin, get the hint and leave!* I swallowed hard, before finally uttering the words that would hurt me as much as they would hurt her. "I'm sorry. I didn't mean to give you the wrong idea. I don't like you ... like that."

Erin flinched. She inhaled sharply and stood tall, though her hands shook. "It's okay." She let out a hollow chuckle. "So stupid of me. Sorry for bothering you with that." She took a step back. "Well, see you around."

"Bye." I waved.

With quick steps, Erin jogged out of the building.

And I buried my head in my hands. Holy fuck, this wasn't right. Every fiber in my body yelled at me to go after her, to grab her arm, to pull her to me, and to kiss her again.

That fucking kiss! It really had been heaven and I craved more.

But I couldn't. I shouldn't.

I really had to stay as far from Erin as I could. Even if I was going to watch over her and protect her, it would have to be done from a distance. She could never see me or know about me.

Feeling like everything around me had taken a miserable turn, I dragged my feet up the stairs and into my room.

In desperate need of a shower to wash off the blood from my skin and the pain from this entire night, I took off my bloodied shirt and threw it in the trash can beside my desk.

Then, I got a glance of me in the mirror hanging from my closet door.

I did a double take.

My jaw hanging open, I approached the mirror and stared at my chest.

A tattoo identical to Erin's lie above my heart.

I gasped, finally realizing it wasn't a tattoo.

It was the sign of a soul bond.

Want more of Erin's and Rey's story? You can grab book 2, The Hunter Secret, now!

THANK YOU

Thank you for reading *The Demon Kiss*!

Reviews are very important for authors. If you liked my book, please consider leaving a review on your favorite retailer and/or on goodreads, please!

You can get the next book in the series now:

The Hunter Secret

Don't forget to sign up for my Newsletter to find out about new releases, cover reveals, giveaways, and more!

If you want to see exclusive teasers, help me decide on covers, read excerpts, talk about books, etc, join my reader group on Facebook: Juliana's Club!

ABOUT THE AUTHOR

While USA Today Bestselling Author Juliana Haygert dreams of being Wonder Woman, Buffy, or a blood elf shadow priest, she settles for the less exciting—but equally gratifying—life as a wife, a mother, and an author. She resides in North Carolina and spends her days writing about kick-ass heroines and the heroes who drive them crazy.

Subscribe to her mailing list to receive emails of announcement, events, and other fun stuff related to her writing and her books: www.bit.ly/JuHNL

For more information:
www.julianahaygert.com

facebook.com/julianahaygert

twitter.com/juliana_haygert

instagram.com/juliana.haygert

goodreads.com/juliana_haygert

pinterest.com/julianahaygert

bookbub.com/authors/juliana-haygert

ALSO BY JULIANA HAYGERT

To find links and more info, go to:

www.julianahaygert.com/books/

Shorts

Into the Darkest Fire

Standalones

Daughter of Darkness

Rite World: Blackthorn Hunters Academy

The Demon Kiss (Book 1)

The Hunter Secret (Book 2)

The Soul Bond (Book 3)

The Shadow Trials (Book 4)

The Infernal Curse (Book 5)

Rite World

The Vampire Heir (Book 1)

The Witch Queen (Book 2)

The Immortal Vow (Book 3)

The Warlock Lord (Book 4)

The Wolf Consort (Book 5)

The Crystal Rose (Book 6)

The Wolf Forsaken (Book 7)

The Fae Bound (Book 8)

The Blood Pact (Book 9)

The Wyth Courts

Winter King (Book 1)

Spring Warrior (Book 2)

Summer Prince (Book 3)

Autumn Rebel (Book 4)

The Fire Heart Chronicles

Heart Seeker (Book 1)

Flame Caster (Book 2)

Sorrow Bringer (Book 3)

Earth Shaker (Novella)

Soul Wanderer (Book 4)

Fate Summoner (Book 5)

War Maiden (Book 6)

The Everlast Series

Destiny Gift (Book 1)

Soul Oath (Book 2)

Cup of Life (Book 3)

Everlasting Circle (Book 4)

Willow Harbor Series

Hunter's Revenge (Book 3)

Siren's Song (Book 5)